Hello,
World!

説著英語
去旅行

+ MP3

Travel, English, and Fun

作者｜Carlos Campbell
審訂｜Judy Majewski

CONTENTS

1

訂機票

DIALOGUE

(A) Hello. I'd like to confirm my reservation. My name is Anne Lin.

(B) What's your name again, please?

(A) L-I-N, Lin.

(B) I see. What's your flight number?

(A) I'm on Flight 724 to London on October 31.

(B) Hold on, please . . . Yes, Flight 724 for London, departing on October 31, is confirmed.

(A) 喂，我叫林安妮，我想再確認之前的訂位。

(B) 麻煩您再說一次您的姓氏。

(A) L-I-N，林。

(B) 了解。請問您是搭哪一個班次？

(A) 10月31日到倫敦的724號班機。

(B) 請您稍候一下。……您預定10月31日飛往倫敦的724號班機，已經幫您確認好了。

Study Points

I'd like to . . .	我想……	這是比較禮貌的說法，意思是「I want to . . .」
flight number	飛機班次	每個航班都按一定規律編訂號碼，以便於區別和管理
on flight 724	搭乘 724 號班機	搭乘飛機，介系詞要用 on
hold on	稍等，不要掛斷	這是電話常用語
depart	出發；離港	相對用法是 arrive（抵達）

PLANE TICKET

PLN

PLN 4155

8 665

機票行程常用語彙

air ticket 機票
e-ticket (= Electronic Ticket) 電子機票
one-way (OW) 單程（票）
round-trip (RT) 來回（票）
circle trip (CT) 環遊票（機票）
round-the-world (RTW) 環球行程（機票）
standby 在機場候補

NA

DES

HOT

NAME

DESTINATION

1 **air ticket** 機票

2 **airlines** 航空公司

3 **electronic ticket** 電子票

4 **flight itinerary** 班機行程

5 **flight number** 飛機班次

6 **reserve**
reservation 訂位

7 **confirm**
confirmation 再確認

8 **cancel**
cancellation 取消

9 **flight connection** 轉機

10 **transfer** 不同航班的轉機

11 **transit** 過境

12 **first class** 頭等艙　13 **business class** 商務艙　14 **economy class** 經濟艙

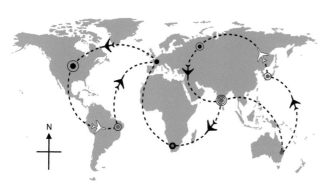

15 **airline code**
航空公司班機代號
16 **airport code** 機場縮寫
17 **city code** 城市縮寫
18 **origin** 起站
19 **destination** 終站
20 **stopover** 停留站

TRAVEL CLASS
客艙級別

代號	級別	說明
F Class	頭等艙	First Class
C Class; J Class	商務艙	Executive Class; Business Class; Dynasty Class
Y Class	經濟艙	Economy Class

不同的艙等（class），有不同的「票價等級」（fare basis）。按國際航空票務規定，經濟艙有 Y、B、M、Q、V、H、L 等七個不同的票價等級。Y 是經濟艙票價等級中的全價票，上述七個艙等中字母越接近左邊（Y）的，表示票價折扣越少；反之，越接近最右邊的（L）的，表示票價折扣越多，機票的限制也越多。

DEPARTURE FLOWCHART
出境流程圖

A

CHECK-IN COUNTER
到航空公司的劃位櫃檯

辦理報到手續

1

搭機時，要往**Departure**（**出境**）走，不要走到**Arrival**（**入境**），然後到所搭乘的航空公司的**劃位櫃檯**（**Check-In Counter**），辦理報到

驗票→託運行李過磅→貼行李標籤（Claim Tag）

行李若超重，須支付超重運費（Overweight Charge/ Excess Baggage Charge）

2

如果想選擇座位，須於此時提出要求：
→靠窗座位：Window Seat
→靠走道座位：Aisle Seat
→中間座位：Middle Seat

3

領取登機證（Boarding Pass）及行李標籤（Claim Tag）。登機證上會記載你的：
→飛機班次：Flight No.
→登機門：Gate No.
→座號：Seat No.

4

依機場規定購買機場稅（Airport Tax）（我國機場稅已內含在機票中）

B

PASSPORT INSPECTION AREA/
PASSPORT COUNTER
護照查驗

將護照及登機證等備妥，
接受查驗。

C

PASSENGER AND
BAGGAGE INSPECTION
旅客及隨身行李檢查

通過「金屬探測器」及
「行李X光」的檢查站。

D

BOARDING GATE
前往登機門

1

登機證上會註明登機門號碼，
接著依指示前往登機門。此時
可利用時間打電話，或到美食
部或免稅商品店逛逛。

2

在登機前半小時到候機室
（Lounge）等候。

E

PLANE
登機

聽到登機廣播後，拿出
登機證以供服務人員查
驗並登機。

1 訂機位 (3)

1 I'd like to book a flight from <u>Hong Kong</u> to <u>Chicago</u> on <u>Tuesday, July 12</u>.
我要訂7月12日星期二從香港飛芝加哥的機票一張。

2 I'd like to book a flight that leaves in the morning.
我要訂一張早上出發的機票。

3 I'd like to reserve a seat for <u>Boston</u> on <u>May 8</u>.
我想訂一張5月8日去波士頓的機票。

4 I'd like to reserve a seat from <u>Los Angeles</u> to <u>Taiwan</u>.
我想訂一張從洛杉磯到台灣的機票。

SENTENCE PATTERNS
基本句型

出發地　目的地　　時間

I'd like to book a flight from <u>Vienna</u> to <u>Seoul</u> on <u>Sunday, July 1</u>.

我要訂一張在 時間 從 出發地 飛往 目的地 的機票。

目的地　　時間

Are there any flights to <u>Frankfurt</u> on <u>August 7</u>?

有在 時間 飛往 目的地 的機票嗎？

機票費用
常用語彙

normal fare 普通票價

full fare (adult fare) 全票（12 歲以上）

half fare (children's fare) 半票（2 至 12 歲，票價為全票的一半）

infant fare 嬰兒票（2 歲以下，票價為全票的 1/10，無座位）

fully booked 客滿

overbooking 超額訂位

5 Are there any flights to <u>Beijing</u> on <u>Sunday</u>?
有星期天飛往北京的機票嗎？

6 Are there any direct flights to Vancouver?
有沒有直飛溫哥華的班機？

7 What time does Flight 724 arrive in Singapore?
724號班機幾點會到新加坡？

8 Which airport do I leave from?
我要去哪一個機場搭機呢？

9 How much is the airfare from Paris to Taipei?
從巴黎到台北的機票是多少錢？

10

Ⓐ When would you like to leave?

Ⓑ ① I'd like a flight on May 15.
② The sooner, the better.

Ⓐ 您要什麼時候走？

Ⓑ ① 我要5月15日出發的班次。
② 可以的話，越早越好。

2 再確認或變更預約

⑪ May I confirm my reservation? 我可以再確認訂位嗎？

⑫ Please confirm my flight. 請幫我再確認之前訂的機位。

⑬ May I have your name and flight number?
請告訴我您的姓名和搭乘的班機號碼。

⑭
Ⓐ Your name, please.

Ⓑ Lily Wu. Wu is my family name.

Ⓐ How do you spell it?

Ⓑ That's W-U, Wu.

Ⓐ I can't find your name on the list.

Ⓑ I made my reservation in Taiwan.
Would you check it again, please?

Ⓐ 麻煩告訴我您的大名。

Ⓑ 我叫吳莉莉，吳是姓氏。

Ⓐ 怎麼拼呢？

Ⓑ W-U，吳。

Ⓐ 名單上沒有您的名字耶。

Ⓑ 我是在台灣訂位的，請您再查查看。

⑮ My name is David Lee. My flight number is BA604 to Sydney on October 2.
我的名字是李大衛，我的班機是10月2日飛往雪梨的BA604號。

⑯ I'd like to confirm the departure time. 我想確認出發的時間。

⑰ By what time should I check in? 我幾點前要辦好登機手續？

18 I'd like to change <u>my reservation</u>. 我想改班次。

19 I'd like to change my flight date from June 5 to June 9.
我想把6月5日的班機為6月9日。

20 I'd like to change a reservation for flight number 212 on March 22. 我想改3月22日212號班機的訂位。

21 Can I change my reservation to an earlier flight?
我可以改搭早一點的班機嗎？

22 Which flights have seats available? 哪一個班機還有位子？

23 I'll go standby. 我在排候補。

landing 降落

takeoff 起飛

runways 機場跑道

control tower 塔台

apron 停機坪

jet bridge;
passenger walkway 空橋

3 在機場辦理登機手續

24 I'd like to check in now. 我現在想辦理登機手續。

25 Please show me the seating plan. 請讓我看座位表。

26 I'd like a window seat, please. 請給我靠窗的位子。

27 I'd like an aisle seat, please. 請給我走道的位子。

28 A seat somewhere in the front, please. 請給我前面的位子。

29 A seat somewhere in the back, please. 請給我後面的位子。

30 I'd like to sit with my friend. 我要和我的朋友坐在一起。

31 Altogether I have two pieces of luggage. 我一共有兩件行李。

32 I'd like to bring this on board. 我這個是要帶進飛機上的。

33　**Ⓐ** Your baggage is overweight. 您的行李超重了。

　　　Ⓑ How much is the extra fare? 那超重要付多少錢？

34 What is the boarding time? 登機時間是幾點？

35 Where is the boarding gate? 登機門在哪裡？

36 What is the gate number for the United Airlines flight to Rome? 聯合航空飛往羅馬的登機門是幾號？

37 Is this the right way to Gate 14? 14號登機門是往這裡走嗎？

38 Where is the duty-free shop? 免稅店在哪裡？

Airport 機場

Shuttle Bus 接駁車

Domestic Terminal 國內線航廈

International Terminal 國際線航廈

Cargo Terminal 貨運站

Arrival Lobby 入境大廳

Departure Lobby 出境大廳

Transit Room 過境室

Connection Counter 轉機櫃檯

Transfer Desk 轉機櫃檯

Information Counter 服務台

Courtesy Room; VIP Lounges 貴賓室

Waiting Room 候機室

Duty-free Shop 免稅商店

Check-in Counter 報到櫃檯

Luggage Scale 磅秤

Baggage Tag 行李牌

Carry-on Baggage 隨身攜帶的行李

Trolley 手推行李車

Security Check 安全檢查

Immigration Office 入出境辦公室

Customs Service Counter 海關服務櫃檯

Animal & Plant Quarantine 動植物檢疫

轉機（flight connection）的方式有三種：

1. 不同航班的轉機（transfer）：轉機的旅客在轉機點（stopover point）下機後，要遵循「Transfer」的標示走到轉機櫃台辦理報到，改搭另一班飛機。

2. 同航班的中途過境（transit）：同一架飛機在途中降落，讓到站的旅客下機，或是讓新搭的旅客上機，而中途不下機的旅客則在飛機上或機場等候起飛。

3. 隔夜轉機（stopover night）：旅客無法在同一天轉機到目的地時，航空公司會提供免費住宿，讓旅客隔天再改搭別的飛機。

轉機
方式

AIRPORT
INFORMATION
BOARD
機場看板
英漢對照

Service Center ℹ️
Car Rental 🚗
Departure ✈️
Check-in 2 🎒

↖
↖

Zuschauerterrasse
Rundfahrten

↓

Parking 🅿️
Regional Bus 🚌
Tramway 🚃
Railway 🚂
Check-in 3 🎒

↗
↗
↘
↘
↘

服務中心 ℹ️
租車 🚗
離境大廳 ✈️
報到櫃檯2 🎒

↖
↖
↖
↖

Zuschauerterrasse
Rundfahrten

↓

停車場 🅿️
本地公車 🚌
電車 🚃
鐵路 🚂
報到櫃檯3 🎒

↗
↗
↗
↘
↘

lobby 大廳

| Arrivals **1-2** ✈ → |
| Departures **1-2** ✈ |
| Check-in **1-16** 🚶 |
| Information **?i** ↰ |

| 入境大廳 **1-2** ✈ → |
| 出境大廳 **1-2** ✈ |
| 報到櫃檯 **1-16** 🚶 |
| 詢問處 **?i** ↰ |

Departure
出境

Arrival
入境

Information Center 詢問處

Customs
海關

Waiting Room
候機室

Pass
通關

Airport Terminal
航廈

Passport Control
護照檢查

Baggage Scanning
行李掃瞄

Weighing of Luggage
行李過磅

Ticket Checking
機票檢查

Control Tower
塔台

X-ray Scanning
機場 X 光檢查

Locker
寄物櫃

Duty-free Shop
免稅商店

PASSENGER TICKET AND BAGGAGE CHECK
SUBJECT TO CONDITIONS OF CONTRACT
Issued by

Date of issue

Carrier ID   ISS. AGT. ID.

Place of Issue

Name of passenger (not transferable)   Fare Basis

From   Carrier/Flight — Class/Date — Time — Res. —

To   Revalidation

Endorsements/Restrictions

Original Issue   Issued in Exchange for

Fare Calculation

Fare   Equiv. Fare Pd.   Form of Payment

Seq. No.   Allow   PCS

Tax/Fee/Charge   PCS. CK. WT. UNCK. WT.

Tax/Fee/Charge   Document Number

Stock Control Number TX

Tax/Fee/Charge

Total   Do Not Mark or Write in the White Area Ab

機票及行李票
根據合約條款
開票公司

開票公司日期
航空公司識別碼   票發單位識別碼

開票地點

票種代碼

旅客姓名（不可轉讓）

出發地   航空公司 / 班機號碼—艙等 / 起飛日期—時間—訂位狀態

目的地   再驗證

禁止背書轉讓 / 其他限制

原始機票   換票變更事項

票價計算

票價   實際付款幣值   付款方式

序號   行李限量   物件數

PCS. CK. WT. UNCK. WT.

機場稅 / 服務費 / 外加稅費   機票編號

機場稅 / 服務費 / 外加稅費

機場稅 / 服務費 / 外加稅費   庫存控制數

票面總金額   請勿在上方白色區塊做記號或寫字

Passenger Coupon

Name of Passenger

Tour Code

—— Invalid Before —— Invalid After

From

To

PIN Code

CONJ. TKT. No.

Carrier/Flight   Class/Date   Time

Gate   Board Time   Seat

CK. WT.   UNCK. WT.

Additional Seat   Information

PCS CK. WT. UNCK. WT. Seq. No. PCS CK. WT. UNCK. WT.

Baggage ID No.
Document No.

AIRPLANE
TICKET
機票
中英對照

旅客存根聯

旅客姓名

團號

——期限之前無效——期限之後無效

出發地
目的地

訂位代號

聯票號碼

航空公司 / 班機號碼 艙等 / 日期 時間

登機門   登機時間   座位

已秤重量   未秤重量

外加座位   資訊
PCS CK. WT. UNCK. WT. Seq. No. PCS CK. WT. UNCK. WT.

行李識別碼
機票編號

2

機艙內

IN THE CABIN

DIALOGUE

Ⓐ Where is my seat?

Ⓑ Your seat number is 16A. Down this aisle, to your right.

Ⓐ Thank you.

Ⓐ Excuse me, but I think you're sitting in my seat.
What's your seat number?

Ⓒ It's 17A. Oh, I'm sorry. I made a mistake.

Ⓐ Don't worry about it.

Ⓐ 請問我的位子在哪裡?

Ⓑ 你的位子是16A,這邊的走道直走,在你右手邊的地方。

Ⓐ 謝謝。

Ⓐ 不好意思,你坐的這個位子好像是我的。請問你的位子是幾號?

Ⓒ 是17A。哎, 對不起,我弄錯了。

Ⓐ 沒事的。

Study Points

down this aisle	沿著走道走	down作介系詞，是「沿著」的意思。
to your right	在你的右手邊	「to one's right」是「在你的右邊」，「to one's left」是「在你的左邊」。
Excuse me, but . . .	不好意思，……	but 後面接相反的意見，翻譯時不用把 but 翻出來。
I made a mistake.	我弄錯了。	用過去式顯示是既成事實。
Don't worry about it.	請別在意。	更簡單的說法是：No problem. That's OK.

一般飛機上的座位都是從前面開始算起1、2、3……，從左邊算起是A、B、C……，登機時請再確定自己的座位號碼。

Visa 簽證
Visa on arrival 落地簽證
Visa-free 免簽證

簽證用語

BOARDING PASS
Passenger Ticket and Baggage Check   First Class

BOARDING PASS
First Class

GATE	GATE CLOSES	SEAT
6	14:35	3B

Class
First Class

Departure
Tokyo

Arrival
New York

Ref No
046 15638 000621

Gate: 6

Gate Closes: 14:35

SEAT
3B

登機證
乘客機票和行李檢查   頭等艙

登機證
頭等艙

登機門	登機門關閉時間	座位
6	14:35	3B

艙等
頭等艙

起飛地
東京

目的地
紐約

參考號
046 15638 000621

登機門： 6

登機門
關閉時間： 14:35

座位
3B

BOARDING PASS
登機證
中英對照

✈ Departures

Time	To	Flight no.	Gate	Remarks
09:35	NEW YORK	DF2753	A1	DEPARTED
09:40	FRANKFURT	LN3211	C3	BOARDING
09:45	TORONTO	GT4638	A2	DEPARTED
09:45	LONDON	KV3323	B4	ON TIME
09:50	MIAMI	LX3100	A2	DELAYED
09:55	SYDNEY	LV2317	A5	ON TIME
10:00	PARIS	BD9032	B1	ON TIME
10:00	OSLO	FB5610	C4	ON TIME
10:05	HONG KONG	EN4267	A4	DELAYED
10:10	BARCELONA	GC5433	C1	ON TIME
10:15	TOKYO	LY4488	B2	ON TIME
10:20	MOSCOW	KF3280	B4	CANCELLED
10:25	ZURICH	TK7252	A4	ON TIME
10:30	LOS ANGELES	TK3946	A1	ON TIME
10:35	ROME	RZ1408	B3	DELAYED
10:40	HONOLULU	EK4319	A1	NEW TIME

✈ 離站時刻表

起飛時間	飛往	航班	登機門	備註
09:35	紐約	DF2753	A1	已起飛
09:40	法蘭克福	LN3211	C3	登機中
09:45	多倫多	GT4638	A2	已起飛
09:45	倫敦	KV3323	B4	準時
09:50	邁阿密	LX3100	A2	延誤
09:55	雪梨	LV2317	A5	準時
10:00	巴黎	BD9032	B1	準時
10:00	奧斯陸	FB5610	C4	準時
10:05	香港	EN4267	A4	延誤
10:10	巴塞隆納	GC5433	C1	準時
10:15	東京	LY4488	B2	準時
10:20	莫斯科	KF3280	B4	取消
10:25	蘇黎世	TK7252	A4	準時
10:30	洛杉磯	TK3946	A1	準時
10:35	羅馬	RZ1408	B3	延誤
10:40	檀香山	EK4319	A1	已更改時間

DEPARTURE BOARD
班機離站時刻表
中英對照

時刻表用語

Departure Board 離站時刻表

Arrival Board 到站時刻表

Estimated Time of Arrival (ETA) 預定抵達時間

Estimated Time of Departure (ETD) 預定離開時間

4 **carry-on baggage** 登機行李

1 **captain** 機長

2 **flight attendant** 空服員

3 **passenger** 旅客

5 **departure** 出境

6 **arrival** 入境

7 **check-in counter** 報到櫃檯

8 **terminal** 航廈

9 **waiting room** 候機室

10 **passport** 護照

11 **boarding pass** 登機證

BOARDING PASS
Passenger Ticket and Baggage Check   First Class

| GATE | BOARDING TIME | SEAT |
| 6 | 14:30 | 3B |

Class
First Class
Departure   Arrival
Tokyo   New York
Ref No
046 15638 000621

BOARDING PASS
First Class

Gate: 6

Boarding
Time: 14:30

SEAT
3B

12 **boarding gate** 登機門

13 **boarding time** 登機時間

14 **seat number** 座號

15 **departure time** 起飛時間

16 **overhead compartment** 頭頂上方置物櫃

17 **emergency exit** 緊急出口

18 **oxygen mask** 氧氣罩

19 **life jacket** 救生衣

20 seat belt light 安全帶警示燈

21 reading light 閱讀燈

22 call button 呼叫鈕

23 blanket 毯子

24 pillow 枕頭

25 lavatory 廁所

26 vacant 空的

27 occupied 使用中

28 airsick 暈機

29 airsickness bag 嘔吐袋

CAUTION SIGNS
飛機上的英文告示

FASTEN SEAT BELT WHILE SEATED
LIFE VEST UNDER YOUR SEAT

STOW CUP HOLDER DURING TAXI, TAKE - OFF AND LANDING

taxi 在這裡當動詞用，是「（飛機）滑行」的意思

乘坐時請繫好安全帶
救生衣置於您的座位下方

飛機滑行、起飛和降落時，請闔上用餐板

機上常見飲料

orange juice 柳橙汁
tomato juice 番茄汁
apple juice 蘋果汁
cola 可樂
sprite 雪碧
diet cola 健怡可樂
orange soda 柳橙汽水
mineral water 礦泉水
oolong tea 烏龍茶

beer 啤酒
red wine 紅酒
white wine 白酒
whiskey 威士忌
gin and tonic 琴湯尼
Bloody Mary 血腥瑪麗
screwdriver 螺絲起子
vodka lime 伏特加萊姆
vodka rum 伏特加蘭姆

1 搭機的用語

1 Excuse me. Can you show me where seat 23D is?
請問23D的座位在哪裡？

2 Excuse me. May I get through? 不好意思，借過一下。

3 Excuse me. Is this seat vacant? 不好意思，這位子有人坐嗎？

4 May I change seats with you? 我可以跟您換位子嗎？

5 Sorry, I think this is my seat. 不好意思，您坐到我的位子了。

6
 Ⓐ Where can I put this bag?
 Ⓑ Please put it in the overhead storage bin.
 Ⓐ 這個行李可以放在哪裡？
 Ⓑ 請放在上面的架子上。

7
 Ⓐ Where can I leave my bag?
 Ⓑ You can place your luggage under the seat in front of you.
 Ⓐ 請問行李可以放在哪裡？
 Ⓑ 您可以把行李放在前面的座位下方。

8 Can you please help me put my bag up there?
可以幫我把行李放上去嗎？

9 May I recline my seat? 我可以把椅背向後仰嗎？

YES **You can make and receive calls on this flight**
Incoming text messages are free To make a call, dial 00 + country prefix + phone number
GSM mobile phones may be used on board but only when the <Phone Use Permitted> sign is illuminated

Boeing 737-800 Safety Information

Emergency oxygen

Seat belts
Fasten seat belts | Undo seat belts

Life vests

Emergency landing

Exit A — doors

Exit B — over wings

Exit A doors | Exit B over wings | Exit B over wings | Exit A doors

YES **您可以在機上接打電話**
收簡訊免費用　　打電話請撥 00 ＋國家冠碼＋電話號碼
〈您可使用電話〉的燈亮時，您在機上可以使用 **GSM** 手機

波音 737-800 安全設施使用方式

氧氣罩的使用

安全帶的使用
緊上安全帶 | 解開安全帶

救生衣的使用

緊急降落措施

出口 **A**—機艙門

出口 **B**—翼上緊急出口

Exit A doors | Exit B over wings | Exit B over wings | Exit A doors

2 機艙內的飲食

10
- Ⓐ What would you like to drink?
- Ⓑ What kind of drinks do you have?
- Ⓐ We have coffee, black tea, orange juice, tomato juice, beer, and wine.
- Ⓑ One tomato juice without ice, please.
- Ⓐ 請問您想喝什麼飲料？
- Ⓑ 有哪些飲料呢？
- Ⓐ 我們有咖啡、紅茶、柳橙汁、番茄汁、啤酒和葡萄酒。
- Ⓑ 請給我番茄汁，不加冰塊。

11 Would you like some coffee or tea? 請問您想要咖啡還是茶？

12 Some more coffee, please. 請再給我一些咖啡。

13
- Ⓐ Which would you like for dinner: beef, chicken, or fish?
- Ⓑ Fish, please.
- Ⓐ 請問您的晚餐想要吃牛肉、雞肉，還是魚肉？
- Ⓑ 我要魚肉，謝謝。

14 May I have a vegetarian meal instead? 請問可以換素食嗎？

15 Can you take my tray? 可以麻煩你把餐盤收走嗎？

16 I am a little hungry. Is there anything to eat?
我有點餓，請問有什麼可以吃的嗎？

17 Do you have any instant noodles? 你們有泡麵嗎？

AIRLINE MEAL
飛機上的餐飲

fried rice 炒飯　　**lasagna** 千層麵

beef 牛肉　　**lamb** 羊肉　　**pasta** 義大利麵　　**fish** 魚肉

SFML	Fish, Seafood	魚；海鮮
ORML	Oriental Meal	東方餐食（葷食）
AVML	Asian Vegetarian Meal	東方素食（無蛋奶、無蔥薑蒜）
VGML	Vegetarian Meal	西式素食（無奶、無蔥薑蒜）
BBML	Baby Meal	嬰兒餐
LSML	Low Sodium (Low-Salt Meal)	低鈉無鹽餐
HNML	Hindu Meal	印度教餐食（無牛肉）
MOML	Muslim Meal	伊斯蘭教餐食（無豬肉）
KSML	Kosher Meal	猶太教餐食（遵守猶太教之規定）

3 用機上的設備 🎧 10

18 May I please have a blanket and a pillow?
請給我毛毯和枕頭。

19 Do you have Chinese magazines or newspapers?
有中文雜誌或報紙嗎？

20 Do you sell tax-free goods on the flight?
機艙內有賣免稅商品嗎？

21 I'd like some water to take my medicine with.
我要吃藥，請給我一杯水。

22 Can I exchange my earphones? They don't work.
這副耳機沒有聲音，我可以換另外一副嗎？

23 How do I turn on the light? 請問要怎麼開燈？

24 I feel like vomiting. I need an airsickness bag.
我想吐。我需要嘔吐袋。

25 I feel sick. Can I have some medicine?
我覺得不舒服，有什麼藥可以給我服用嗎？

26 May I have some airsickness medicine? 請問有暈機藥嗎？

27 Would you mind checking on her?
可以請你看看她怎麼了嗎？

28 Is there a doctor on board? 飛機上有醫生嗎？

(11) Ladies and gentlemen, this is Flight Attendant Andrea Simpson speaking. On behalf of Air Garden Airlines, I would like to welcome you aboard Flight AG203 from San Francisco to Taipei. The flight time today is 10 hours and 30 minutes. Our expected time of arrival is 9:10 a.m. local time, July 7.

各位先生女士，我是空服員 Andrea Simpson，謹代表空中花園航空公司，歡迎各位搭乘從舊金山飛往台北的AG203班機。飛行時間預計是10小時30分鐘，我們預計會於台北當地時間7月7日上午9點10分抵達。

(12) Good evening, passengers. This is your captain speaking. Welcome to Flight AG203, nonstop from San Francisco to Taipei. The weather ahead is good, and we should have a smooth flight. The time is 7:20 p.m. The cabin crew will be coming around in about twenty minutes to offer you a light snack and beverage. I'll talk to you again before we reach our destination. If you have any questions about our flight, please don't hesitate to ask one of our flight attendants. Relax and enjoy the flight. Thank you.

各位旅客，晚安，我是機長，歡迎搭乘從舊金山直飛台北的AG203班機。飛行天候良好，我們預計可以有一趟順利的飛行。現在時間是晚上7點20分，20分鐘之後，將會有空服員為您提供點心和飲料。在我們抵達目的地之前，我會再跟大家報告。如果您對此航班有任何問題，請儘管詢問我們的空服員。請放鬆來好好享受這趟飛行，謝謝！

(13) We are approaching an area of turbulence. For your safety and comfort, please go back to your seats and fasten your seat belts. Please keep your belts fastened until the "Seat Belt" sign goes off. Thank you.

本班機正接近亂流區，為了讓各位旅客能安全、舒適地度過，請各位旅客回到座位上，繫上安全帶，直到「繫上安全帶」的燈號熄滅為止，謝謝。

3

入境

IMMIGRATION

DIALOGUE

A What's the purpose of your visit?

B Sightseeing.

A How long are you going to stay in the United States?

B For seven days.

A Where will you be staying?

B I'll stay at the Hilton Hotel.

A Do you have your return ticket?

B Yes. Here it is.

A 你來此的目的是什麼？

B 觀光。

A 你打算在美國停留多久？

B 七天。

A 你要住在哪裡？

B 我住希爾頓大飯店。

A 你有回程的機票嗎？

B 有的，在這裡。

Study Points

the purpose of your visit	此行目的	進入這個國家的目的
sightseeing	觀光	sightseer 則是指「觀光客」
Where will you be staying?	你會住在哪裡？	也可以説成： ① Where are you going to stay? ② Where will you stay?
return ticket	回程機票	來回機票是 round-trip ticket
Here it is.	東西在這裡。	把東西交給別人時，可以説： ① Here it is. ② Here you are.

入境手續

1 入境審查（immigration inspection）

準備好護照和入境申請表（disembarkation card），有時也會被要求附上回程機票。審查人員可能會詢問你的入境目的、居留時間、住宿地點、持有多少現金等問題。

2 提領行李（baggage claim）

辦完入境手續後，就可以到行李提領處領取自己的行李。如果找不到行李，可以向工作人員出示行李牌（claim tag），請他們幫忙尋找。

3 海關檢查（customs inspection）

須出示護照及關稅申報表，海關人員會問是否需要申報物品，有時會要求打開行李接受檢查。在接受入境檢查或海關檢查時，回答應該具體且明確。

1 **arrival time** 到站時間

2 **arrival terminal** 到站航廈

3 **arrival hall** 入境大廳

4 **baggage hall** 行李提取大廳

5 **baggage claim** 行李提領

6 **lost & found** 遺失行李詢問處

7 **passport control** 護照檢查

8 **immigration** 入境審查

9 **immigration form; disembarkation card** 入境申請表

10 **immigration inspection**
入境檢查

11 **customs** 海關

12 **customs control** 海關管制

13 **customs inspection** 海關檢驗

14 **customs declaration form**
海關申報表

15 **customs duties** 關稅

16 **declare** 申報

17 **cash** 現金

18 **tax-free articles**
免稅品

19 **prohibited articles**
違禁品

20 **cigarette** 菸

21 **liquor** 酒類飲料

22 **time difference** 時差

23 **jet lag** 時差失調

37

Bag Claim
Ground Transport
Parking
Rental Cars
Information

← All Gates

提領行李
陸地交通

停車場
租車
服務處

所有登機門

↑ Baggage hall
Arrivals hall
Passport control

↑ 行李大廳
入境大廳
護照檢查

美國入境須知

美國政府為防範恐怖分子，從 2004 年 10 月 26 日起，實施 US-VISIT 安檢系統，要求入境之外國旅客於入關時掃描十指的指紋，以查驗身分。美國移民官員如果懷疑入境者之身分、證件或來美之目的，可以拒絕旅客入境，並予以遣返。入境美國應誠實申報隨身所攜帶之財物，不可攜帶違禁物品，如申報不實或未申報，物品有可能被沒收，或遭受民、刑事處分。以下是一些相關規定：

01 個人隨身攜帶入境物品（含商品及禮品）之免稅額，美國居民為 800 美元，非美國居民為 100 美元；酒類免稅額為一公升（攜帶者須年滿 21 歲）；菸類免稅額為一條菸，或五十枝雪茄，或二公斤菸草。古巴出產之雪茄及香菸禁止攜入。

02 禮物不應包裝，以便海關檢查。

03 可攜帶之現金及證券額度為一萬美元。超過額度者，須事先向海關申報，倘若未先行申報而經查獲者，將遭受民、刑事懲罰，現金及證券亦將被沒收。

04 旅客不得攜帶管制農（畜）產品及動物入境美國，倘若未申報而經查獲者，除該產品將被沒收外，並可能被處以罰金。

1 入境審查方面的問答 🎧16

1
- Ⓐ May I see your passport, please?
- Ⓑ ① Here it is.
  - ② Here you are.
- Ⓐ 請出示護照。
- Ⓑ 好的，在這裡。

---

2 What is the purpose of your visit? 你此行目的是什麼？

3
- ① Just sightseeing.
- ② I've come for sightseeing.
- ③ I'm here as a tourist. 觀光。

4
- ① On business.
- ② I'm here on business. 出差。

---

5 Half for business and half for pleasure.
一半是為了工作，一半是旅遊。

6
- ① I'm here as a foreign student.
- ② I'm here to attend a university. 我是來留學的。

---

7 I've come to study at a language school.
我是來語言學校唸書的。

---

8 To visit a friend. 來拜訪朋友的。

GETTING THROUGH CUSTOMS
海關常問的問題

① Welcome to America. May I see your passport, please? — 歡迎您來美國。可以請您讓我看您的護照嗎？

② Where are you coming from? — 您是從哪個國家來的？

③ What is the purpose of your visit? — 您此行的目的是什麼？

④ How long are you planning to stay? — 您打算停留多久？

⑤ Where will you be staying? — 您會住在哪裡？

⑥ Do you have anything to declare? — 您有東西要申報嗎？

❾

Ⓐ ① How long are you going to stay?
  ② How long do you plan to stay?

Ⓑ ① I'll be here for three weeks.
  ② About two weeks.
  ③ A couple of months.

Ⓐ 你打算停留多久呢？

Ⓑ ① 三個星期。
  ② 大約兩個星期。
  ③ 兩、三個月。

10

Ⓐ ① Where are you going to stay?

② Where will you stay?

Ⓑ ① At the Hilton Hotel downtown.

② I'll stay with a friend in New York.

③ I'll be staying with my younger sister's family.

④ I'll be staying at my friend's home.

Ⓐ 你打算住在哪裡？

Ⓑ ① 我打算住在市中心的希爾頓大飯店。

② 我會住在我紐約朋友的家中。

③ 我會住在我妹妹那裡。

④ 我會去住我朋友家。

11

Ⓐ How much money do you have?

Ⓑ About $1,000.

Ⓐ 你帶了多少現金？

Ⓑ 大約1,000塊美金。

12 Do you have your return ticket? 你有回程機票嗎？

13

Ⓐ May I see your return ticket?

Ⓑ ① Here it is.

② This is my return ticket.

Ⓐ 麻煩給我看你的回程機票。

Ⓑ ① 好的，在這裡。

② 這是我的回程機票。

2 提領行李

14

A Where is the baggage claim area for Flight 212?

B It's number 7.

A 請問212號班機的行李在哪裡提領？

B 在7號。

---

15 I can't find my luggage. 我找不到我的行李。

---

16 My luggage is missing. 我的行李不見了。

---

17 Here is my claim tag. 這是我的行李牌。

18

A What kind of bag is it?

B ① It's a green suitcase.

② It's about this size.

③ It's a medium-sized suitcase with my name tag on it.

A 是什麼樣的行李？

B ① 是個綠色的手提箱。

② 大概是這個尺寸的大小。

③ 是中型的手提箱，行李牌上有我的名字。

---

19 How soon will you deliver my luggage?
我的行李大概什麼時候會到？

---

20 Please deliver my luggage to the Hilton Hotel.
麻煩你把行李送到希爾頓大飯店。

---

21 My suitcase is badly damaged. 我的手提箱嚴重受損了。

3 與海關人員的對答 🎧 18

22
- Ⓐ Do you have anything to declare?
- Ⓑ ① No, I have nothing to declare.
  ② I have something to declare.
  ③ Just this.
- Ⓐ 你有什麼要申報的物品嗎？
- Ⓑ ① 我沒有要申報的物品。
  ② 我有要申報的物品。
  ③ 只有這個要申報。

23
- Ⓐ What is their approximate value?
- Ⓑ About $120.00.
- Ⓐ 這些物品的價值大約是多少？
- Ⓑ 大約是120塊美金。

24 You'll have to pay duty on this. Please declare this at the window over there.
這個物品是要課稅的，請到那邊那個窗口去申報。

25 It's a souvenir for my friend. 是要給朋友的紀念品。

26 It's for my personal use. 是我的私人用品。

27
- Ⓐ Do you have any liquor or cigarettes?
- Ⓑ I have two bottles of whiskey.
- Ⓐ 你有攜帶酒或香菸嗎？
- Ⓑ 我有帶兩瓶威士忌。

28　Ⓐ　Do you have any fruit or vegetables?

　　Ⓑ　I have this box of fruit. It's a gift.

　　Ⓐ　你有攜帶水果或蔬菜嗎？

　　Ⓑ　我有帶一箱水果，是送人的禮物。

29　I'm sorry. You're not allowed to bring in fruit.

很抱歉，水果是禁止攜帶入境的。

30　OK. You can pass through.

好了，沒問題，你可以通行了。

台灣出入
境須知

❶　入境可以帶幾條菸？幾瓶酒？超過數量時要如何處理？

旅客須滿20歲以上，入境時每人限帶捲菸200支，或雪茄25支，或菸絲1磅。
酒1公升為限，超過的數量應向關稅局申請辦理課稅。

❷　我可以帶多少台幣及美金入出境？

① **新台幣**：60,000元為限，如超過限額，應在入境或出境前事先向中央銀行
申請核准；超額部分未經核准，不准攜入或攜出。

② **外幣**：攜帶外幣入境不予限制，但超過等值美金10,000元現金者，應報明
海關登記，未經申報依法沒入。

③ **人民幣**：20,000元為限。如超過限額，雖向海關申報，仍僅能於限額內攜
出；如申報不實，超過部份，依法沒入。

④ **有價證券**：總面額逾等值10,000美元者，應向海關申報。未依規定申報或
申報不實者，科以相當於未申報或申報不實之有價證券價額之罰鍰。

⑤ **黃金**：不予限制，但應於入、出境時向海關申報，如總額超過美金20,000
元，應向經濟部國際貿易局申請輸入許可證，並辦理報關驗放手續。

4 兌換錢幣

CHANGING CURRENCY

DIALOGUE

ⓐ Can you change this into dollars?

ⓑ How would you like it?

ⓐ I'd like ten twenties, five tens, and the rest in change.

ⓑ Certainly, sir.

ⓐ By the way, how much is the commission?

ⓑ One percent.

ⓐ 請把這個換成美金。

ⓑ 請問要換哪些種類的面額？

ⓐ 我要20塊美金的10張、10塊美金的5張，剩下的請換成零錢。

ⓑ 先生，好的。

ⓐ 對了，手續費是多少？

ⓑ 百分之一。

Study Points

change . . . into . . .	將……兌換成……	也可以説： • change . . . to . . . • change . . . for . . .
How would you like it?	要換哪幾種面額？	兌換外幣時，常會被問到這個問題。
ten twenties, five tens	20 塊的 10 張、10 塊的 5 張	紙鈔是 bill，銅板是 coin
How much is the commission?	手續費是多少錢？	commission 是「佣金」

一般在機場、車站的銀行兌換處，或是市區銀行、飯店等地方，都可以兌換外幣，但是以下有幾點要特別注意的地方是：

1 機場、車站和飯店的匯率都比市區銀行要來得高，所以在這些地方最好只要兌換小金額就好，如果兌換的金額大的話，到市區的銀行兌換較為划算。

2 因為每次兌換錢幣都會收取手續費，所以最好減少兌換的次數。

3 因為零錢無法再兌換，因此最好能全部用完。

4 兌換剩餘的當地貨幣時，需要出示兌換證明書，所以要保管好。

5 兌換旅行支票時會用到護照，所要先準備好。

1 currency exchange counter 貨幣兌換處

2 currency 通貨；流通貨幣

3 foreign currency 外幣

4 cash 現金

5 bill 紙幣

6 coin 硬幣；錢幣

7 small change 零錢

8 check 支票

9 traveler's check
旅行支票

10 signature 簽名

11 exchange rate 匯率

12 exchange receipt 兌換證明

13 commission 手續費

14 ID card 身分證

15 bankbook 存摺

16 account 戶頭

17 savings account 儲蓄帳戶

18 deposit account 存款帳戶

19 checking account 支票帳戶

1 兌幣時的用語

1 Where can I change money? 兌換處在哪裡？

2 Where is the nearest bank? 最近的銀行在哪裡？

3 I'd like to change NT dollars into US dollars.
我想把台幣兌換成美金。

4 Can you change American dollars into British pounds?
可以幫我把美金換成英鎊嗎？

5 Can you break this into small change?
可以幫我把這些錢換成零錢嗎？

6 Can you break this $100 bill?
可以幫我把這100塊美金換成零錢嗎？

7 Please include some small change. 請同時換些零錢。

8 Five tens, ten fives, and the rest in quarters, please.
請給我5張10塊美金、10張5塊美金，其餘的換成25分錢的硬幣。

9 I'd like it all in twenties, please. 請全部換成20塊美金。

10 Can you please cash this check and give me ten twenty-dollar bills and twenty five-dollar bills?
請將這張支票換成10張20塊的美金，以及20張5塊的美金。

美元銅板

1 cent（分）
5 cents
10 cents
25 cents
50 cents
1 dollar
（口語為buck）

英鎊銅板

1 penny（便士）
2 pence
5 pence
10 pence
20 pence
50 pence
1 pound
（口語為quid）

歐元銅板

1 cent
2 cents
5 cents
10 cents
20 cents
50 cents
1 euro

11 Please cash this one hundred-dollar check.
請把這張100塊美金的支票換成現金。

12 Can you break it down like this?
（將紙條拿給對方看）請照這張紙上所寫的方式換錢。

13 What's the exchange rate for euros?
歐元的兌換匯率是多少？

14 What commission do you charge? 手續費是多少錢？

15 Can I have an exchange receipt? 請給我交易收據。

16 The amount of money is not right. 這金額錯了。

⑫ Cash machine

ATM
(= automatic teller machine)
自動提款機

2 匯款或開戶的用語

⑰ I'd like to get a remittance from Taiwan.
我想領台灣寄來的匯款。

⑱ How can I get a remittance from Taiwan?
我要怎麼領取台灣寄來的匯款？

⑲ I'd like to transfer some money. 我想要匯款。

⑳ I'd like to open an account. 我想要開戶。

㉑ Will you tell me how to open a savings account?
你可以教我怎麼開戶嗎？

㉒
Ⓐ What kind of account would you like to open?
Ⓑ A savings account, please.
Ⓐ 你要開哪種戶頭呢？
Ⓑ 我要開活期存款的戶頭。

㉓ I'd like to make a deposit. 我想要存款。

㉔ I'd like to withdraw $400 from my account.
我想從戶頭提出400塊美金。

BANK VOCABULARY
銀行常用動詞

1	open an account	開戶頭
2	close an account	結清戶頭
3	deposit money	存錢
4	make a deposit	存錢
5	withdraw money	提錢
6	cash a check	兌現支票
7	apply for a loan	申請貸款
8	borrow money	借錢
9	lend money	放款
10	purchase	買進
11	speak to the manager	找經理談
12	check my account balance	查戶頭餘額
13	transfer money	轉帳

DIALOGUE

Ⓐ I'd like to check in, please. The name is Louis Lee.
I made a reservation from Taiwan.

Ⓑ Just a moment, please. Yes, Mr. Louis Lee, a single room for three nights. Is that right?

Ⓐ Yes, that's right.

Ⓑ Would you like to pay in cash or with a credit card?

Ⓐ Cash, please.

Ⓑ Will you fill out this form, please?

Ⓐ 我要辦住房手續。我是來自台灣的李路易斯，我有訂房。

Ⓑ 請稍等。李路易斯先生，您是訂三個晚上的單人房，是嗎？

Ⓐ 是的，沒錯。

Ⓑ 您要用現金付款，還是用信用卡付？

Ⓐ 我要用現金。

Ⓑ 請填寫這張表格。

Study Points

I'd like to check in, please.	我要辦住房手續。	check in 的名詞是 check-in
made a reservation	已預約	reservation 的動詞是 reserve
a single room for three nights	三個晚上的單人房	single room 也可以說成 single
pay in cash or with a credit card	付現還是刷卡	刷卡也可以說「pay by credit card」
fill out this form	填寫這個表格	fill out 指「填寫」（表格等）

在飯店辦理住宿手續的慣用說法是：

- **I'd like to check in, please.**
- **Check in, please.**

然後再告訴對方自己的名字，以及有事先訂房：

My name is . . . I have a reservation.

這時櫃檯會從訂房名單中找出你的名字，並且給你一份住宿單，請你登記一些基本資料。寫的時候最好能確定房間的種類（single、double、twin）、費用及住宿的天數等，最後再領住房卡就行了。

當我們進入到飯店的房間，整個人一下子就會鬆懈下來。有人可能感覺像回到家一樣，不知不覺中製造出意想不到的麻煩。以下舉出幾點在歐美的飯店中應注意的事項。

1 要給幫我們提行李的 bellboy（旅館的侍者）或 porter（大飯店搬運行李的服務生）小費。通常一件行李是給一塊美金，給小費的時候記得要跟對方說聲謝謝。

2 即使人待在房間裡也要鎖門。如果有人敲門，不要將房門全部打開，應先問對方是誰：「Who is it?」等確定好是誰之後再開。有些人就是因為沒有弄清楚就隨便開門而遭到搶劫。

3 最常發生的問題，就是把鑰匙放在房間裡，忘記帶出來。因為飯店房間的門幾乎都是屬於自動上鎖的，因此只要離開房間就一定要記得帶鑰匙。萬一真的被關在門外，只好去跟櫃檯的人員說：「I'm locked out.」請他們來幫你開門。

4 就算房門上了鎖，也不見得絕對保險。像現金或是平時不需要用到的護照等貴重物品，除了放在保險箱，也可以詢問櫃檯人員是否幫忙保管：「Will you keep my valuables?」

5 只有在飯店裡的房間內，才是屬於自己私人的空間，所以只要踏出了房門，就要注意自己的儀容。千萬不要穿著睡衣走出房間，或是在走廊上大聲喧嘩。

6 如果你不希望被人打擾，想睡晚一點的話，可以將「DO NOT DISTURB」的牌子掛在門外。如果外出時希望有人來清掃房間，則可以掛上「PLEASE MAKE UP THE ROOM」的牌子。

飯店組織圖

1 Front Office 客務部

Reservation 訂房
Reception 櫃檯接待
Operator 總機
Cashier 出納（屬財務部 Financing）
Business Center 商務中心
Service Center; Concierge 服務中心
· Doorman 門衛
· Bellhop 行李員
· Driver 駕駛
· Flight Greeter 機場接待

2 Housekeeping 房務部

Housekeeping 房務組
　　（又稱 Room Maid 房務人員）
Cleaning 清潔組（負責公共區域）
Laundry Room 洗衣房
Linen Room 布巾室（房務部的心臟地帶）
Lost and Found 遺失物品管理
Florist 花房
Butler 客房值勤服務員（管家服務）

3 F & B (Food & Beverage Department) 餐飲部

Dining 餐廳部
Kitchen 廚房
Steward 餐務部（餐具管理、廢棄物管理）
Room Service 客房餐飲

Front of the House
前場
房客可接觸的區域

Security 安全室（門禁管制、停車場管理）
Engineering 工程部
Purchasing 採購部
Sales & Marketing 行銷業務部
Financing 財務部
Human Resources 人力資源部
Public Relations 公關部
Information 資訊部

Back of the House
後場
房客不可進入的區域

1 hotel 飯店；旅館

2 motel 汽車旅館

3 Villa 渡假村旅館

4 Youth Hostel 青年旅館

5 Bed & Breakfast 民宿

6 Spa 水療飯店

7 lobby 大廳

8 front desk;
reception desk 櫃檯

9 doorman 門衛

10 receptionist 櫃檯人員

11 operator 總機人員

12 bellhop; porter 行李員

13 room attendant 客房服務員

14 **reservation** 訂房

15 **check-in** 辦理住房

16 **checkout** 辦理退房

17 **housephone** 內線電話

18 **morning call; wake-up call** 晨喚服務

19 **room (meal) service** 客房餐飲服務

20 **hanger** 衣架

21 **closet** 衣櫃

22 **safety box** 保險箱

23 **bathrobe** 浴袍

24 **refrigerator** 冰箱

hotel charges 住宿費
extra charge 額外費用
bill 帳單
receipt 收據
amount 金額
service charge 服務費
dining charge 餐費

single room 單人房

twin room 雙床房

double room 雙人房
＊在美國，double room
有時也指 twin room 喔

triple room 三人房

suite 套房

presidential suite 總統套房

1 飯店的預約

1 I'd like to reserve a hotel room for tonight.
我想訂今晚的客房。

2 Do you have a room available for tomorrow night?
你們明天晚上有空房嗎？

3 Is there a room available for Wednesday and Thursday nights? 星期三和星期四晚上有空房嗎？

4 I'd like to stay for three nights. 我想住三個晚上。

5 Do you have a twin room? 你們有空的雙人床房間嗎？

6 What kind of room do you have in mind?
你想住什麼樣的房間？

7 I'd like a double room. 我要一間雙人房。

8 I'd like a single room with a bath. 我要有含衛浴設備的房間。

9 How much is it per night? 住宿一晚要多少錢？

10 How much is a single room? 單人房是多少錢？

11 Is there a room that costs about $60 a night?
有沒有一晚60塊美金左右的客房？

12 Does the price include breakfast? 費用有含早餐嗎？

room with a balcony 有陽台的房間　　bayview suite 灣景套房

⑬ Does that include tax and service charges?
費用包含稅及服務費嗎？

⑭ Do you have any cheaper rooms? 有沒有便宜一點的房間？

⑮ I'd like a room with a nice view. 我要一間視野比較好的房間。

⑯ I'd like a quiet room. 麻煩給我一間比較安靜的房間。

⑰ I'll take that room. 我要訂那個房間。

⑱ What time can I check in? 我什麼時候可以辦住宿手續？

2 辦理住宿登記

⑲ I'd like to check in, please. 我要辦理住宿手續。

⑳ My name is Jeremy Wilson. I have a reservation.
我叫傑洛米‧威爾森，我有訂房。

㉑ I have a 3-day reservation starting today.
我訂了三天的房間，從今天開始算起。

㉒ I've reserved a superior suite. 我訂了一間高級套房。

23 I made a reservation in Taiwan. 我已經在台灣訂好房間了。

24 Here is my confirmation slip. 這是訂房的確認書。

25
Ⓐ I'm sorry, we don't have your reservation.

Ⓑ I'm sure I have a reservation. Can you try to find my name again?

Ⓐ 抱歉，我們的訂房單上沒有您的名字。

Ⓑ 我確定我有訂房，可以請你再找找看是否有我的名字？

26 I don't have a reservation. Is there a room available tonight? 我沒有訂房，請問今晚還有空房嗎？

27 I'd like a single room for two nights.
請給我一間單人房，要住兩晚。

28 I'm sorry, but we are full. 抱歉，我們已經客滿了。

29 Unfortunately, all the singles are booked. But we still have a few doubles left.
抱歉，單人房都已經客滿了，我們只剩下幾間雙人房。

30 How much is the room charge? 房間的費用是多少？

31 Would you fill out this registration card? 請填寫住宿單。

32 When is checkout time? 退房的時間是幾點？

33 Will you carry my luggage to my room?
你可以幫我把行李搬到房間去嗎？

3 櫃檯

34 Will you keep my valuables? 可以幫我保管貴重物品嗎？

35 Can you tell me how to use the safety box?
請告訴我保險箱的使用方法。

36 Where is the emergency exit? 安全門在哪裡？

37 Where is the dining room? 餐廳在哪裡？

38 What time does breakfast start? 早餐幾點開始？

39 Will you keep my key? 可以幫我保管鑰匙嗎？

40 May I have the key to room 215? 請給我215號房的鑰匙。

41 Please airmail this letter. 請幫我把這封信用航空郵件寄出。

42 I'd like to send a fax to Taiwan. 我想傳真到台灣。

43 Are there any messages for me? 有沒有我的留言？

44 Can you tell me how to use the housephone?
請告訴我內線電話的使用方法。

elevator 電梯

emergency exit 緊急出口

4 客房服務

45 This is Room Service. May I help you?
這裡是客房服務中心，需要為您服務嗎？

46 This is room 1126. I'd like to order a ham sandwich and a cup of coffee.
這是1126號房，請幫我送來一份火腿三明治和一杯咖啡。

47 I'd like to order breakfast for tomorrow.
我想訂明天的早餐。

48 Please bring some ice and water. 請幫我送冰塊和水。

49 Please bring me a blanket. 請幫我送一條毛毯。

50 I'd like a bath towel. 我想要一條浴巾。

51 This is room 807. Would you give me a wake-up call?
這裡是807號房，可以請你給我morning call嗎？

52 Would you give me a wake-up call at 7 a.m.?
明天早上7點請給我morning call。

No Smoking 禁止吸菸

Swimming Pool 游泳池

DO NOT DISTURB
請勿打擾

MAKE UP ROOM
請打掃房間

Laundry Room 洗衣房

5 洗衣服務

53 I have some laundry. Do you have laundry service?
我有要清洗的衣物，請問有洗衣的服務嗎？

54
Ⓐ When will it be ready?
Ⓑ By tomorrow evening.
Ⓐ 什麼時候可以洗好？
Ⓑ 明天晚上。

55 Can you clean my suit for me by tomorrow morning?
明天早上以前可以幫我把西裝洗好嗎？

56 I need to have my laundry done as quickly as possible.
我的衣物需要盡速送洗。

6 住宿時遇到的麻煩

57 This is not the room I asked for. 這和我想訂的房間不一樣。

58 The room next door is too noisy. 隔壁的房間很吵。

59 I'd like to get a different room, please. 我想換房間。

60 The room light doesn't work. 房間的電燈壞了。

61 Something's wrong with the air conditioner. 空調有問題。

62 I can't get any hot water in the bathroom. 浴室沒有熱水。

63 The toilet doesn't flush. 馬桶的水沖不出來。

64 The toilet seems to be blocked. 馬桶好像阻塞了。

65 My room hasn't been cleaned. 我的房間還沒打掃。

66 There are no bath towels. 沒有浴巾。

67 I've locked myself out. 我忘記帶鑰匙了。

68 I lost the room key. 我把鑰匙弄丟了。

7 退房的說法

69 I'm going to leave tomorrow morning. 我明天早上離開。

70 I'd like to stay one more night. 我想再多住一晚。

71 I'm going to leave early tomorrow morning. Please have my bill ready. 我明天一早要離開,所以請先準備好帳單。

72 I'd like to check out now. Can you take my luggage down?
我現在要辦退房,可以麻煩你把我的行李拿下來嗎?

73 I'd like to check out, please. 我要辦退房。

74 My bill, please. 麻煩幫我結帳。

75 I had two bottles of beer and a cola from the refrigerator.
我喝了冰箱裡的兩瓶啤酒和一瓶可樂。

76 What's this charge for? 這是什麼費用?

77 I think there's a mistake in this bill. 這帳單好像算錯了。

78 Do you accept traveler's checks? 可以用旅行支票嗎?

79 Can I pay by credit card? 可以用信用卡付款嗎?

80 Can you keep my luggage until five o'clock?
可以幫我保管行李到5點嗎?

81 I left something in my room. 我有東西放在房間裡忘記拿了。

82 Will you call me a cab, please? 可以幫我叫輛計程車嗎?

6 餐廳

DIALOGUE

ⒶMay I take your order?

ⒷA beer, steak with French fries, and the chef's special salad.

ⒶHow would you like your steak?

ⒷWell-done, please.

ⒶYes. And what kind of dressing on your salad?

ⒷThousand Island dressing, please.

Ⓐ請問您要點菜了嗎？

Ⓑ我要一瓶啤酒、牛排、薯條和主廚沙拉。

Ⓐ請問牛排要幾分熟？

Ⓑ我要全熟的。

Ⓐ好的。那麼請問沙拉醬要用哪一種醬？

Ⓑ請給我千島醬。

Study Points

May I take your order?	決定要點什麼了嗎？	這是服務生詢問客人點餐時的常用說法
How would you like your steak?	您的牛排要幾分熟？	「How would you like...」用來詢問對食物的喜好或品嚐結果
Well-done, please.	我要全熟的。	well-done 指「全熟」
What kind of dressing on your salad?	您要哪一種沙拉醬？	常見的沙拉醬有法式沙拉醬、義式沙拉醬和千島醬等

到國外旅行，令人期待的活動之一就是「用餐」了。如果你只是一直擔心自己會不會點餐，不知道要怎麼吃異國料理，或是用餐禮節應該如何等等，那你就無法盡情享受異國風味的美食了。

為了能有個美好的用餐經驗，我們先來學習餐飲方面的基本用語吧。在餐廳裡，如果不知道該如何點餐，不妨直接問服務生：

What do you recommend? 有什麼要推薦的餐點呢？
What's today's special? 今天的特餐是什麼？

如果已經準備好點餐，你可以說：

I'll have . . . 我想要點……
I'll take . . . 我想要點……
I'd like . . . 我想要點……
. . ., please. 請給我……

Table Etiquette
餐桌禮儀

勿擅自自行入內

- 進入餐廳大廳之後，不要隨便地走進去，要先告訴入口處的服務人員，説明你是否有事先訂位以及用餐人數，等服務人員安排好位子之後再進去。
- 入座時，要用右手拉椅子，並從左側入座，並記得説「女士優先」。

用餐時的禮儀

- 喝湯時勿出聲。即使湯很燙，也不要做出把湯吹冷的樣子。
- 不要一邊吃東西，一邊説話。
- 勿將盤子舉起或是靠在嘴上。
- 刀、叉若是掉在地上，可請服務生幫忙撿起來，不要自己去撿。
- 避免討論低俗的話題。
- 如果你拿不到鹽或是胡椒時，可以跟坐在附近的人説：「Pass me the salt, please.」請他們幫忙傳遞，不要自己伸手去拿。
- 不要互相分菜。

刀叉的使用順序

- 餐桌上的刀叉是依照上菜順序由外向內排列的，所以使用的順序也是一樣，先從最外面的餐具開始使用。
- 用餐中若想將刀、叉放在餐盤上，以「八」字型擺放，結束用餐時則一律靠右排放。

喝咖啡、喝茶的正確動作

NEVER ALWAYS NEVER ALWAYS

Dessert Spoon
Cake Fork
Bread and Butter Plate
Bread and Butter Knife

點心匙
點心叉
麵包奶油盤
麵包奶油刀

魚叉
主餐叉
沙拉叉
盤子
端菜盤用的大盤子

Fish Fork
Dinner Fork
Salad Fork
Plate
Service Plate

Water Glass
Red Wine Glass
White Wine Glass

開水杯
紅酒杯
白酒杯

海鮮叉
湯匙
茶匙
魚刀
主菜刀
沙拉刀

Oyster Fork
Soup Spoon
Teaspoon
Fish Knife
Dinner Knife
Salad Knife

1 plate 盤子 **2** napkin 餐巾

6 chopsticks 筷子

5 bowl 碗

3 fork 叉子 **4** knife 刀子

7 spoon 湯匙

8 salt 鹽 **9** pepper 胡椒

12 mustard 芥末

10 ketchup 番茄醬 **11** mayonnaise 美奶滋

16 syrup 糖漿

13 vinegar 醋 **14** soy sauce 醬油 **15** chili sauce 辣椒醬

jam：由整顆果醬製成，有果粒

jelly：由果汁製成，質地較稀，無果粒

17 peanut butter 花生醬

18 jelly 草莓醬

19 beef 牛肉

20 lamb 羊肉

21 pork 豬肉

22 chicken 雞肉

23 sausage 香腸

24 seafood 海鮮

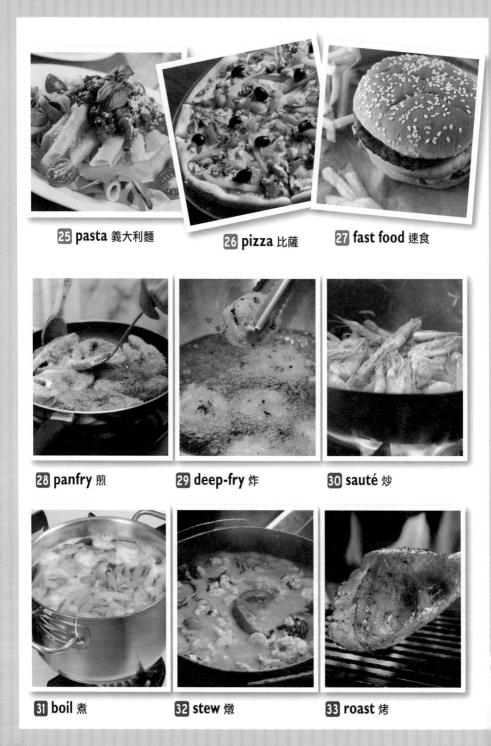

25 pasta 義大利麵

26 pizza 比薩

27 fast food 速食

28 panfry 煎

29 deep-fry 炸

30 sauté 炒

31 boil 煮

32 stew 燉

33 roast 烤

RESTAURANT SIGNS
餐廳招牌

Cafeteria 自助餐

Bar & Restaurant 酒吧餐廳

Fast Food 中式快餐店

BUFFET

Buffet 歐式自助餐廳

Coffee Shop 咖啡廳

Stop and Eat Here!
聞香下馬，入內享用！

spaghetti
義大利肉醬麵

1 找餐廳 (34)

❶ Can you recommend a good restaurant near here?
可以告訴我這附近有好吃的餐廳嗎？

❷ Where can I find the best local food?
在哪裡可以吃到好吃的當地料理呢？

❸ I'd like to try a typical dish of this country.
我想吃這個國家特有的菜。

❹ Are there any seafood restaurants around here?
這附近有海鮮餐廳嗎？

❺ Do you know of any nice, inexpensive restaurants?
你知道哪裡有便宜又好吃的餐廳嗎？

❻ I'd like a good restaurant with reasonable prices.
我想找價格合理又好吃的餐廳。

❼ I'd like to have some real Italian food.
我想吃點道地的義大利菜。

西餐上菜順序

1 aperitif 餐前酒

2 appetizer 開胃菜

3 soup 湯品

4 main course 主菜

5 salad 沙拉

6 dessert 甜點

7 coffee/tea 咖啡或茶

2 訂位

8

Ⓐ I'd like to reserve a table for two at seven tonight.

Ⓑ I'm sorry, but it's full at that time. Can you make it at 8:00?

Ⓐ I'm afraid I can't. Thank you, anyway.

Ⓐ 我想訂今天晚上七點、兩個人的位子。

Ⓑ 很抱歉,那個時段已經客滿了,請問您要不要訂八點的呢?

Ⓐ 那就不用了,謝啦。

9 I'd like to make a reservation, please. 我要訂位。

10 Do I have to be formally dressed? 一定要穿正式的服裝嗎?

11 Should I wear a tie? 需要打領帶嗎?

12 The name is Lin. We have a reservation for 7 o'clock.
我姓林，我訂了七點的位子。

13 We don't have a reservation. Do you have a table for four?
我們沒有訂位，請問有四個人的位子嗎？

14 Can we have a table? 有空位嗎？

15

(A) I'd like a table for three, please.

(B) Sorry, but our tables are full now. Can you wait for a while?

(A) About how long do we have to wait?

(B) I think it's about 30 minutes.

(A) All right. We'll wait.

(A) 我要三個人的位子。

(B) 很抱歉，目前剛好客滿，可以請您稍等一會嗎？

(A) 大概要等多久呢？

(B) 大約30分鐘左右。

(A) 好吧，我們要等。

16 May we wait for a table? 我們可以等位子嗎？

17 Are you serving lunch now? 現在開始供應午餐了嗎？

18 Can we have a table by the window?
我們可以坐靠窗的位子嗎？

19 We'd like seats near the street. 我們想要靠街道的位子。

4 點餐

⑳ Excuse me. May I see the menu? 不好意思，請給我看菜單。

㉑ Would you show me a wine list? 請給我看酒類的菜單。

㉒ What do you recommend? 有沒有什麼菜色要推薦的？

㉓ What's today's special? 今天的特餐是什麼？

㉔ Which dish does the chef recommend?
主廚推薦的料理是哪一個？

㉕ ① Do you have a table d'hôte?
② Do you have the fixed meal of the day? 有套餐嗎？

㉖ What can you serve quickly? 有什麼是可以立刻上菜的？

㉗ What is this like? （指著菜單）這是什麼料理？

㉘ What kind of drinks do you have? 有哪些飲料？

㉙ What kind of drinks do you have for an aperitif?
有什麼餐前酒？

㉚ Do you have a house wine? 有自釀酒嗎？

㉛ Excuse me. May I order now? 不好意思，我要點餐。

㉜ I'm ready to order. 我要點餐。

㉝ I'll start with a beer. 請先給我一杯啤酒。

㉞ A bottle of red wine, please. 麻煩給我一瓶紅酒。

35

Ⓐ May I take your order?

Ⓑ Just a moment, please. I haven't decided yet.

Ⓐ 決定好要點餐了嗎?

Ⓑ 請等一下,我還沒決定好。

36

Ⓐ Are you ready to order?

Ⓑ Let me think for a moment.

Ⓐ 決定好要點餐了嗎?

Ⓑ 請讓我考慮一下。

37 I'll have this and this. (指著菜單)請給我這個和這個。

38 I'll have the same. 我也點跟他(指同行者)一樣的。

39 Can I have the same dish that he is having?
(指著別桌的菜)請給我跟他一樣的菜。

40 I'll take today's special. 我點今天的特餐。

41 How would you like your steak? 請問牛排要幾分熟?

42 I'd like a seafood salad. 請給我一盤海鮮沙拉。

43 I'll start with chicken consommé. 麻煩先給我清燉雞湯。

44 I'll have the sirloin steak with mashed potatoes.
麻煩給我沙朗牛排加馬鈴薯泥。

45 What's the garnish? 食物上裝飾的是什麼?

46　Ⓐ What kind of dressing would you like on your salad?

　　Ⓑ Thousand Island dressing, please.

　　Ⓐ 請問您的生菜沙拉要加哪一種醬？

　　Ⓑ 請給我千島沙拉醬。

47　I'll have coffee after dinner. 餐後請給我咖啡。

48　I'd like ice cream for dessert. 餐後點心我要點冰淇淋。

49　I'll order dessert later. 餐後點心待會兒再點。

50　I'll pass on the dessert. 餐後點心不用了。

rare 一分熟	medium-rare 三分熟	medium 五分熟	medium-well 七分熟	well-done 全熟
僅牛排的表面煎熟呈褐色，內裡的肉微暖，呈血紅色，刀切下時會有帶點血水。	牛排的表面呈褐色，中間部分的肉溫溫的，呈紅色。	牛排外圍呈褐色，中間的肉呈粉紅色，中心部分溫熱，但仍可見一絲絲血紅色。	中間部分的肉呈褐色，中心溫熱，外圍成稍暗紅色，中心部分略呈現粉紅色。	整塊牛排完全熟透，並稍微烤焦。無血水，只有肉汁，肉呈淡褐色。

5 用餐

(38)

51 May I change my order? 我可以更改已點的餐點嗎？

52 My order hasn't come yet. 我點的東西還沒來耶。

53 I didn't order this. 我沒有點這個。

54 This is not what I ordered. 這和我點的東西不一樣。

55 I'm afraid this is a little undercooked. 這個好像沒熟。

56 I dropped a fork. May I have another one?
我的叉子掉了，可以再給我一支新的叉子嗎？

57 Can you bring me the pepper? 可以幫我拿胡椒粉過來嗎？

58 Can you pass me the salt?
（對別的客人説）可以請您把鹽遞給我嗎？

59 Can I have a glass of water? 可以給我一杯水嗎？

60 May I see the menu again? 可以再給我菜單嗎？

61 I'd like to have more bread, please. 請再給我一些麵包。

62 I'd like another beer, please. 請再給我一瓶啤酒。

63 Take this away, please. 請把這個收走。

64 Can I take this home? 我可以把這個打包回家嗎？

65 May I have a doggy bag? 請給我打包用的袋子。

6 結帳付款

66 May I have my bill, please? 我要結帳。

67 Can I pay at the table? 我可以直接在這裡結帳嗎？

68 Where is the cashier? 收銀台在哪裡？

69 Separate checks, please. 我們要各付各的。

70 Let's split it today. 今天各付各的。

71 I'll take care of the bill. 由我來付。

72 ① This is my treat.
② This is on me. 這次我請客。

73 How much is it altogether? 總共多少錢？

74 Does that include the tip? 有含服務費嗎？

75 I think there's a mistake in the bill. 這帳單好像算錯了。

76 Can I pay with this credit card? 可以用這張卡付款嗎？

77 Can I have a receipt? 可以給我收據嗎？

7 速食、簡餐 🎧40

78 Two hamburgers and two small colas, please.
我要兩個漢堡和兩杯小可。

79 Will you be eating here? 您要內用嗎？

80
- **A** (Is this) For here or to go?
- **B** For here, please.
- **A** 內用，還是外帶呢？
- **B** 我要內用。

81 I'd like carryout [takeout]. 我要外帶。

82 Would you like ketchup or mustard on that?
請問要加番茄醬，還是芥末醬嗎？

83
- **A** How would you like your eggs?
- **B** Sunny-side up, please.
- **A** 請問您的蛋要多熟？
- **B** 我要只煎一面的不熟荷包蛋。

84 I'd like a cup of coffee and a pancake. 請給我咖啡和鬆餅。

85
- **A** Cream and sugar?
- **B** Just cream, please.
- **A** 要加奶精和糖嗎？
- **B** 只要加奶精就好了。

hard-boiled egg
全熟水煮蛋

medium-boiled egg
半熟水煮蛋

soft-boiled egg
不熟水煮蛋

sunny-side up
只煎一面
蛋黃不熟

over easy
兩面都煎
蛋黃不熟

over medium
兩面都煎
蛋黃半熟

over hard
兩面都煎
蛋黃全熟

scrambled eggs
炒蛋

omelet
西式蛋餅

poached egg
無殼水煮蛋

8 酒吧

86 Is there room at the counter? 吧檯有空位嗎？

87 What would you like to drink? 請問要喝什麼嗎？

88 Whiskey and water, please. 請給我威士忌加水。

89 I'd like a Scotch on the rocks. 請給我蘇格蘭酒加冰塊。

90 Give us three shots of bourbon, please.
麻煩給我三杯波旁威士忌。

91 Two beers, please. 請給我兩瓶啤酒。

92 Ⓐ What brand?

 Ⓑ Budweiser, please.

 Ⓐ 要點什麼牌子的？

 Ⓑ 請給我一瓶百威。

93 What's your special cocktail? 你們的特調雞尾酒是哪一種？

94 I'll have a martini. 我要一杯馬丁尼。

95 Do you have any snacks? 有點心嗎？

96 May I have another one, please? 請再給我一杯。

97 I'll buy you a drink. 我請你喝一杯。

tumbler
平底無腳酒杯

goblet
高腳杯

beer mug
啤酒杯

white wine glass
白葡萄酒酒杯

red wine glass
紅葡萄酒酒杯

shot of vodka
伏特加酒杯

whiskey glass
威士忌酒杯

brandy glass
白蘭地酒杯

sherry glass
雪莉酒酒杯

champagne flute
笛型香檳杯

champagne saucer
寬底香檳杯

highball glass
海波杯

Collins glass
可林杯

old-fashioned glass
古典杯

cocktail glass
雞尾酒杯

7

購物

SHOPPING

DIALOGUE

Ⓐ I'm looking for a blouse. How much is this blouse?

Ⓑ It's on sale now for just $30.49.

Ⓐ May I try it on?

Ⓑ Sure. The fitting room is over there. . . How is it?

Ⓐ I like this, but it's a bit too big. Do you have a smaller one?

Ⓑ Yes, we do. Here you are.

Ⓐ This fits perfectly. I'll take it.

Ⓐ 我想買襯衫。請問這件要多少錢？

Ⓑ 這件正在打折，打完折後是美金30塊49分錢。

Ⓐ 我可以試穿嗎？

Ⓑ 可以，試衣間在那裡。……穿起來感覺怎麼樣？

Ⓐ 我很喜歡，但是它稍微大了一點。有再小一點的嗎？

Ⓑ 有的，在這兒。

Ⓐ 這件剛剛好，我要買這件。

Study Points

It's on sale.	特價中	「出售中」是 for sale
May I try it on?	可以試穿嗎？	try on 是「試穿」
Do you have a smaller one?	有小一號的嗎？	相反句是：Do you have a bigger one?
This fits perfectly.	這件剛剛好。	衣服、首飾或鞋子，都可以用這句話來表達尺寸適合
I'll take this.	我要買這個。	take 是「買下」

「購物」是海外旅行的一項樂趣，在出發購物之前，最好先調查大型的購物中心、百貨公司和大賣場等的種種情報，因為歐美有許多商店在星期天都是不營業的。這方面的資料也可以向旅客服務中心，或是飯店櫃檯洽詢。

在國外逛街買衣服，走進商店時，店員通常都會走過來親切地和你打招呼，問你：

May I help you? 需要幫忙嗎？

What can I do for you? 有什麼可以幫忙的嗎？

Are you looking for something? 您想找什麼商品嗎？

如果你只是想逛逛而已，就可以客氣地跟她說聲：

I'm just looking. 我只是看看而已。

I'm just browsing. 我只是逛逛而已。

善用免稅的權利

海外旅行的一大樂趣，就是找到國內沒有賣的物品，或是買到比國內還要便宜的東西，甚至可以要求店員打折，充分享受購物殺價的樂趣，你可以用英語對店員說：

Can you give me a discount? 可以算便宜一點嗎？

在歐洲，因為有免稅制度，所以可以退還稅金。以英國為例，除了免稅商店之外，外國旅客在其他商店，只要購買一定的金額，就會被要求加上額外的稅金（VAT, Value Add Tax），但只要透過一些手續，這些外加的稅金還是可以退還回來的。例如，英國的 VAT 是 15 ％，但是每個國家的 VAT 匯率都不一樣，所以最好事先調查清楚。如果你要辦理退稅的話，那付款前就要先跟店員說：

I'd like to buy it under the value added tax system.
我買這個想退稅金。

出示護照和機票之後，店方會把印有這家店名的信封和相關表格交給你，你只要在出境的時候，將護照及表格拿給海關人員檢查，如果沒問題的話，海關人員就會在表格上蓋章，然後你就可以到機場的退稅窗口辦理退稅手續，這樣就可以領到退稅的錢了。

如果你是在無法退現金的國家退稅，那就只要把表格放進信封內，並在海關處投至專用的信箱裡，回國之後就可以領到退稅的金額了。至於退款的方式是要郵寄支票，還是匯到信用卡的戶頭裡，這在你申請退稅的表格上就得先選好了。

像美國對國外的旅客就沒有免稅的制度，因為各州的稅率不同，所以在稅金較低的州購買比較划算喔！

我想買……

I'm looking for . . .
I'd like . . .
I'd like to buy . . .
I want to buy . . .

+

a pair of sneakers

a pair of glasses

a sweater

some dresses

some shirts

ACCESSORIES

TOPS

SKIRTS & DRESSES

TROUSERS

HEELS

ACCESSORY	配件
SKIRT	短裙
DRESS	洋裝
HEELS	高跟鞋
TOP	上衣
TROUSERS	褲子

1 **shopping center** 購物中心

2 **department store** 百貨公司

3 **supermarket** 超市

4 **convenience store** 便利商店

5 **drugstore** 藥妝店

6 **cashier** 收銀台

7 escalator 電扶梯

8 elevator 電梯

9 window 櫥窗

10 cart 購物推車

11 on sale 特價中

12 discount 折扣

1 尋找商店或賣場

1 Is there a department store around here?
這附近有百貨公司嗎？

2 Where's the most famous department store?
最有名的百貨公司在哪裡？

3 Can you tell me where the nearest shopping area is?
可以告訴我最近的商店街在哪裡嗎？

4 Is there a duty-free shop near here?
這附近有免稅商店嗎？

5 Is there a souvenir shop around here?
這附近有販賣紀念品的商店嗎？

6 Where is the drugstore? 藥妝店在哪裡呢？

7 Where is the nearest supermarket?
離這裡最近的超市在哪裡？

8 Where's the ladies' department? 女裝的賣場在哪裡？

9 Where's the bookstore? 書籍的賣場在哪裡？

2 選購與採買 🎧 45

10
- Ⓐ Hello. May I help you?
- Ⓑ I'm looking for a sweater.
- Ⓐ 歡迎光臨。請問您需要什麼嗎？
- Ⓑ 我要找毛衣。

---

11 I'd like to see some watches. 我想看手錶。

---

12 Which brand do you recommend?
請問哪個牌子比較好？

---

13 I want to buy some lipstick. Do you have Revlon products?
我想買口紅，有露華濃的牌子嗎？

---

14 May I look at this? 我可以看一下這個嗎？

---

15 Will you show me something else? 還有沒有別的樣式？

---

16 I'd like to see this in a different fabric.
我想看看別種紋路的。

---

17 Do you have one that's a little bigger?
有沒有大一點的？

---

18 Do you have anything cheaper? 有沒有更便宜一點的？

---

19 What is this made of? 這是什麼材質做的？

---

20 Is this made of leather? 這是真皮的嗎？

3 詢問價錢與殺價

21 How much is it? 多少錢？

22 How much does it cost? 多少錢？

23 How much is it altogether? 全部多少錢？

24 How much for one? 一個多少錢？

25 What's the price [cost] of this bag? 這個皮包多少錢？

26 Does the price include tax? 這個價格含稅嗎？

27 That's too expensive. 那太貴了。

28 Could you give me a discount? 可以打個折嗎？

29 Can't you make it a little cheaper? 可以再算便宜一點嗎？

折扣

新品

SALE

NEW PRICE 打折價　HOT PRICE 特價　NEW PRODUCT 新貨　BEST SELLER 熱賣

Buy now! FANTASTIC CLEARANCE OFFER
STARTS MONDAY, FOR ONE WEEK ONLY

馬上行動！
令人心動的
清倉大拍賣
星期一開始拍賣　僅此一週

4 購買與否、付款和包裝 🎧47

30 I like this. I'll take it. 這個不錯。我要這個。

31 I can't find what I want. 我找不到想買的東西。

32 Can I pay by traveler's check?
可以使用旅行支票付帳嗎？

33 Do you take MasterCard? 你們收萬事達卡嗎？

34 Can I have a receipt, please? 請給我收據。

35 I'm afraid I was shortchanged.
你們找的零錢好像不夠。

36 Would you wrap it, please?
可以幫我包裝嗎？

37 Please wrap it up. 請包裝。

38 Will you wrap these separately, please?
請分開包裝，好嗎？

CLOSED
Hours of Operation:
Mon-Sat 11-7
Sun 12-5
or by appointment

休息中
營業時間：
星期一到星期六 11-7
星期天 12-5
或可預約時間

5 買衣服

39 I want a jacket. 我想買外套。

40 Can you show me the sweater in the window?
可以給我看櫥窗裡的毛衣嗎？

41
Ⓐ What size do you wear?
Ⓑ I'm not sure. Can you take my measurements?
Ⓐ 您是穿幾號的？
Ⓑ 我不太清楚耶，可以幫我量嗎？

42 What is this made of? 這件衣服的材質是什麼？

43 May I try it on? 可以試穿嗎？

44 May I try this jacket on? 這件夾克可以試穿嗎？

45 Where's the fitting room? 試衣間在哪裡？

46 It's too small for me. Do you have a larger one?
這件太小了，有更大一點的嗎？

47 It's too loose. 這件太鬆了。

48 It's a little tight in the waist. 腰的地方有點緊。

49 This fits me perfectly. 這件剛剛好。

50 This is too loud for me. Do you have a plain one?
這件對我來說太豔了，有沒有素一點的？

51 Can you show me one in a lighter color?
可以讓我看看稍微淡一點的顏色嗎？

52 Do you have any other styles? 還有其他款式嗎？

53 Is this washable? 這件可以水洗嗎？

54 Will this shrink if it's washed in cold water?
這件用冷水洗的話會縮水嗎？

55 Will you adjust the length? 可以修改長度嗎？

6 買貴金屬飾品 (49)

56 Will you show me that ring, please?
可以給我看那枚戒指嗎？

57 The second one from the right. 從右邊數過來的第二個。

58
ⓐ What kind of stone is this?
ⓑ It's an opal.
ⓐ 這是什麼寶石？
ⓑ 這是貓眼石。

opal

59 I'd like to see some ruby rings. 我想看紅寶石的戒指。

60 How many karats is this? 這個幾克拉？

61

Ⓐ Is this necklace gold?

Ⓑ Yes, 18-karat gold.

Ⓐ 這條項鍊是金的嗎？

Ⓑ 是的，它是18K金的。

62 Do you have pierced earrings? 有穿耳的耳環嗎？

63 Does it come with a guarantee? 有附保證書嗎？

7 買鞋的用語 (50)

64 I want some black leather shoes. 我想買黑色皮鞋。

65 What sort of leather is this? 這是什麼皮做的？

66 I'd like to try on these shoes. 我想試穿這雙鞋。

67 I'm not sure of my size. 我不知道我的尺寸。

68 Do you have these same shoes one size larger?
有再大一號的這種款式嗎？

69 This pair fits me perfectly. 這雙很合腳。

70 Do you have the same size in red?
同樣大小的有紅色的嗎？

8 買化妝品

71 Do you carry Chanel perfumes? 你們有賣香奈兒的香水嗎？

72 What's a popular perfume? 哪一種香水最暢銷？

73 I want eau de cologne. 我想買古龍水。

74 I want to buy a lipstick. I'd like a rose color.
我想買口紅，要玫瑰色系的。

75 I'd like to try this lipstick color. 我想試這個顏色的口紅。

76 Do you have any lighter colors? 有再淡一點的顏色嗎？

77 Please show me some nail polish. 請給我看指甲油。

78 Do you have a foundation for summer?
有夏天用的粉底嗎？

blush 粉餅

powder puff 粉撲

foundation 粉底

brush 粉刷

mascara 睫毛膏

lipstick 口紅

郵局

POST OFFICE

DIALOGUE

- Ⓐ I'd like to send this letter to Taiwan.

- Ⓑ Airmail or sea mail?

- Ⓐ How long will it take by airmail?

- Ⓑ It should take four or five days by regular airmail and two or three days by special delivery.

- Ⓐ Then send it by special delivery, please. And I'd like 20 of the 50-cent stamps.

- Ⓑ That'll be $12.30, please.

- Ⓐ 我想寄這封信到台灣。

- Ⓑ 你要寄航空的，還是海運？

- Ⓐ 寄航空信多久會到呢？

- Ⓑ 普通郵件是四到五天，快捷郵件則是二到三天會到。

- Ⓐ 那我要寄快捷郵件。另外，我還要買20張50分錢的郵票。

- Ⓑ 這樣總共是$12.30。

Study Points

send this letter	寄這封信	信件的英文，美式是 mail，英式是 post
Airmail or sea mail?	要寄航空還是海運？	海運也可以説 surface mail
How long will it take?	要花多久的時間？	花費多少時間，動詞要用 take
by special delivery	快遞	快遞也可以説 express delivery 或 express mail
50-cent stamps	50 分錢的郵票	量詞作形容詞時要用單數形，所以用 50-cent，而不是 50 cents

現在國際電話或手機漫遊非常方便，抵達飯店後，就可以直接打電話回國，但是如果能寄些國外的風景明信片回國，或是親自寫信給國內的友人，會別有一番情意。

在國外寄郵件，一般在明信片或是信上貼好郵票，交給飯店的櫃檯就可以。但如果要寄包裹或是掛號，那就需要跑一趟郵局囉。

105

1 post office 郵局

2 mailbox 郵筒

3 stamp 郵票

5 letter paper 信紙

4 envelope 信封

6 postcard 明信片

7 parcel; package 包裹

8 sender 寄件人

9 addressee 收件人

106

11 **sea mail** 海運

10 **airmail** 空運

12 **registered mail** 掛號信

13 **express delivery** 快捷

14 **fragile; breakable** 易碎的

FRAGILE
易碎品

KEEP AWAY FROM WATER
避免潮濕

THIS WAY UP
向上

HANDLE WITH CARE
小心輕放

常見的紙箱標示

1 郵局窗口 (54)

❶ Which window is for mail service?
請問寄信的窗口在哪裡？

❷ Which window is for registered mail?
寄掛號信的窗口是哪一個？

❸ At which window can I mail this package [parcel]?
寄包裹的窗口是哪一個？

❹ I'd like to send this by airmail. 這封信我要用航空郵件寄。

❺ By sea mail, please. 我要寄海運。

❻ I'd like to send this by express mail. 這個要寄快捷。

❼ Please send this by special delivery. 這個要寄快遞。

❽ Please send this letter by registered mail.
這封信要寄掛號。

❾ I'd like to send this as printed matter. 這個請當印刷品寄。

❿ What is the fastest way to send this?
用什麼方式寄會最快抵達？

⓫ I'd like to send this the quickest way.
我這個想用最快的方式寄送。

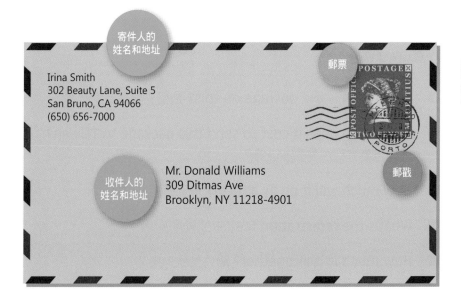

Irina Smith
302 Beauty Lane, Suite 5
San Bruno, CA 94066
(650) 656-7000

Mr. Donald Williams
309 Ditmas Ave
Brooklyn, NY 11218-4901

12 What is the cheapest way to send this?
哪一種郵寄方式的費用最便宜？

13 I'd like to send a money order to Honolulu.
我想寄匯票到檀香山。

14 Can I cash this postal money order?
這張郵政匯票可以換成現金嗎？

15
Ⓐ I'd like to send a package to Taiwan.

Ⓑ What's in this?

Ⓐ All clothes.

Ⓐ 我想寄包裹到台灣。

Ⓑ 這裡面裝什麼？

Ⓐ 都是衣服。

2 詢問費用

16 How much is the postage on this? 這個郵資是多少錢？

17 How much does it cost to send this package to Taiwan?
這個包裹寄到台灣要多少錢？

18 How much will it be by airmail? 寄空運要多少錢？

19 What's the registration fee? 掛號費是多少？

20 How much is it altogether? 總共是多少錢？

21 How much is the postage to Taiwan?
寄到台灣的郵資要多少錢？

22 How much will it cost to send this? 寄這個要多少郵資？

23 Twelve thirty-cent stamps, please. 我要12張30分錢的郵票。

24 I'd like five fifteen-cent stamps, ten twenty-five-cent
stamps, and twenty postcards, please.
我要買5張0.15元和10張0.25元的郵票，還要20張明信片。

25 Can you give me fifteen aerograms?
我要買15張航空郵簡。

如果要從國外寄明信片或包裹回台灣，建議在出國之前，先上中華郵政的網站（http://www.post.gov.tw/post/index.jsp）查詢自己家裡的英文地址。如果已經到了國外，不知道該怎麼寫台灣的住址，那也可以用中文寫地址，最後再加上 Taiwan, R.O.C.。

3 詢問所需時間

26 How long will it take by sea mail?
寄海運的話，要多久才會到？

27 When will it get to Taipei? 什麼時候會寄到台北？

28 How long will it take to get to Taipei? 寄到台北要多久？

29 Will it get there in one week? 一週內會到嗎？

4 其他的表達方式

30 I'd like to have this package insured.
這個包裹我想加掛保險。

31 I'd like to insure this package for $200.
這個包裹我想保險200塊美金。

32 What is the maximum coverage? 最高的賠償金額是多少？

33 Is there a weight limit? 有重量的限制嗎？

34 Do I need to fill out a customs declaration form?
我需要要填寫海關申報表嗎？

35 May I have a customs declaration form?
可以給我一張海關申報表嗎？

36 How do I fill in this declaration form?
我要怎麼填寫這張申請表呢？

9 交通工具

DIALOGUE

Ⓐ Excuse me. I'd like to go to the Bronx Zoo, but what's the best way to get there?

Ⓑ Let me see. You can take a bus, but the quickest way is to take the subway from here.

Ⓐ Where is the nearest subway station?

Ⓑ You can see Manhattan Station over there. The zoo is about a 10-minute walk from the East Tremont Avenue station.

Ⓐ You have been a great help. Thank you for your kindness.

Ⓐ 不好意思，我要去布隆克斯動物園，請問要怎麼去最快呢？

Ⓑ 嗯，你可以搭公車去，但是最快的方法是搭地鐵。

Ⓐ 那最近的地鐵車站在哪裡？

Ⓑ 就在那邊，那是曼哈頓站。到了東崔蒙大道站，下車再走10分鐘左右就到動物園了。

Ⓐ 真是太好了，謝謝你的幫忙。

Study Points

What's the best way to . . .?	去……最好的方式是什麼？	這句話是用來詢問如何搭乘交通工具
You can take a bus.	你可以搭公車去。	take＋交通工具，指搭乘
Where is the nearest . . .?	最近的……在哪裡？	後面直接接地點
10-minute walk	10 分鐘的走路路程	walk 在這裡做名詞用。

一般車票都會以距離和旅遊時間來區分，以下是常見的幾種票種：

❶ 單程票（Single Ticket）如果只到某地，之後不會再搭車，買單程票就是最划算的選擇。

❷ 來回票（Return Ticket）如果回程確定了，建議在買票時就買來回票，通常比兩張單程票便宜，亦可省下再次買票的麻煩。

❸ 區間票 如果只在某個區域活動，可買此票種，如搭乘倫敦地鐵遊覽倫敦，就可買Zone 1與Zone 2兩區的週票，可在使用期限內於該區內任何站隨意進出。巴黎的地鐵也有此票種。

❹ 一日票（One-Day Pass; Daily Pass; One-Day Travel Card）如果想在某地到處觀光，一天內會不斷出入地鐵站，此票種方便又划算。

❺ 週票及月票（Weekly Pass & Monthly Ticket）若待在某地時間較長，可根據停留時間購買週票或月票，有的會要求附一張照片以貼在車票上。

TRAIN TICKET

ONE-WAY TICKET

CLASS	ADULT	CHILD
STD	2	NIL

FROM ...... SAMPLE
TO .... TEXT

DATE .. 21.04.2012
DEP ..... 11:24 AM
ARV ..... 20:38 PM

PRICE ..... 86.50$

No. 1592763005

TRAIN TICKET
INTERNATIONAL TRANSPORTATION OF SAMPLE STATE

CLASS	ADULT	CHILD
BSN	2	1

FROM SAMPLE CITY | TO EXAMPLE CI

DATE 24.02.12 | DEP 18:15 PM | ARV 20:38 28.0

PRICE

SUBWAY SYSTEM
各國地鐵

美國	**Subway**	有些城市（如洛杉磯）的地鐵稱為Metro或Metro Rail，或直接標示「M」。

英國	**Underground/Tube**	英國地鐵的歷史最古老，因為在地底下如管子一般交錯，所以又稱Tube。在英國，subway是指地下道，找地鐵站時可千萬別走錯。

法國	**Metro**	上車時，須自行拉桿或按鈕，門才會開。臺北捷運稱Taipei Metro，但門為電控制開啟。

日本	**Subway/Metro**	日本許多大城市都有不同的地鐵或火車，交通方便。

香港	**MTR**	在香港搭乘地鐵時，可同時購買八達通卡，搭乘公車、渡輪、地鐵時都可使用。

DIRECTION
方向說明

- ① over there 在那裡
- ② next to 在……旁邊
- ③ in front of 在……前面
- ④ opposite 在……對面
- ⑤ on your right;
  on the right-hand side 在右手邊
- ⑥ on your left;
  on the left-hand side 在左手邊
- ⑦ behind;
  at the back of 在……後面
- ⑧ at the corner of 在……轉角處
- ⑨ go straight on 直走
- ⑩ at the corner 轉角處
- ⑪ turn right 右轉
- ⑫ turn left 左轉

block 街區

next to the drugstore
在藥妝店隔壁

bank
銀行

on your right
在右手邊

go two blocks
穿過兩條街

drugstore
藥局

turn right
右轉

turn left
左轉

at the traffic light
在紅綠燈處

at the corner
在轉角

Will you take me to the bank?

I'll tell you how to get there.

go straight on
直行

1 **taxi stand** 計程車招呼站　　**2** **meter** 計費表

3 **fare**（交通）費用　　**4** **trunk** 後行李廂　　**5** **safety belt** 安全帶

6 **traffic lights** 紅綠燈　　**7** **intersection** 十字路口　　**8** **crosswalk** 斑馬線

9 bus station 公車站

10 railroad station 火車站

11 route map 路線圖

12 platform 月台

13 timetable 時刻表

14 ticket window 售票口

15 ticket machine
自動售票機

16 gate 剪票口

17 conductor 列車長

1 搭計程車

1 Where is the taxi stand? 計程車招呼站在哪裡？

2 Where can I catch a taxi? 在哪裡可以招到計程車？

3 There's a taxi stand over there. 那裡有個計程車招呼站。

4 Can you call a taxi for me? 請幫我叫輛計程車，好嗎？

5
Ⓐ Where to?

Ⓑ To the Plaza Hotel, please.

Ⓐ （計程車司機）要去哪裡？

Ⓑ 到廣場飯店。

6 How long does it take to get to the airport?
到機場要多久？

7 About how much is the fare to the airport?
到機場大概要多少錢？

8 Please put this luggage in the trunk.
請把這個行李放在行李廂。

9 To the Central Hotel, please. 麻煩你到中央飯店。

10 To this address, please. 請到這個地址。

11 Please take me to this place. （給司機看地圖）請到這個地方。

TAXI FARE

$2.50	INITIAL CHARGE
40¢	Per 1/5 Mile
40¢	Per 2 Minutes Stopped/Slow Traffic
$1.00	Weekday Surcharge 4pm - 8pm
50¢	Night Surcharge 8pm - 6am

計程車計費標準

起跳費用 $2.50
續程　　　40¢／0.5 英里
延滯計時 40¢／2 分鐘

平日加成 $1.00 (4 pm - 8 pm)
夜間加成 40¢ (8 pm - 6 am)

⑫ The traffic is very heavy now. The subway would be quicker.
現在交通很擁擠，搭地鐵會比較快。

⑬ I'm in a hurry. Would you hurry, please?
我在趕時間，可以開快一點嗎？

⑭ I have to get there by six. Could you hurry along, please?
我要在六點以前到，可以請你開快一點嗎？

⑮ I've got to be at the airport by 5:30. Can we make it?
我五點半以前要到機場，來得及嗎？

⑯ Can I get to the station by 3 o'clock? 三點以前能到車站嗎？

⑰ How much longer will it take? 還要多久？

⑱ Turn to the left, please. 請往左轉。

⑲ Please stop in front of the hotel. 請在飯店前面停車。

⑳ Stop on this side of the next intersection, please.
請在下一個交叉路口靠邊停車。

21　① Stop here, please.

　　② Let me off here, please. 請在這裡讓我下車。

22　① How much is it?

　　② How much is the fare? 多少錢？

23　Thank you. Keep the change. 謝謝，不用找零錢了。

24　This is for you. Thank you. 謝謝，這是小費。

25　May I have a receipt? 可以給我收據嗎？

2 搭公車

26　Where is the nearest bus stop? 最近的公車站牌在哪裡？

27　Do you have a bus route map? 你有公車路線圖嗎？

28　I'd like to go to Manhattan, but which bus should I take?

　　我想去曼哈頓，應該搭哪一路公車呢？

29　What number is the bus for Hollywood?

　　到好萊塢要搭幾號公車？

30　When is the next bus for Chicago?

　　往芝加哥的下一班公車是幾點？

31　How often do the buses run to Chicago?

　　往芝加哥的公車幾分鐘發車一次？

32　What time is the last bus? 末班車是幾點？

33 Does this bus go to National Airport?
這輛公車會開往國際機場嗎？

34 How much does it cost to go to Chicago?
到芝加哥要多少錢？

35 Where should I transfer to get to Soho?
去蘇活區要在哪裡轉車？

36 Where do I get off to go to City Hall?
去市政府要在哪裡下車呢？

37 I'd like to get off at Central Park. 我想在中央公園下車。

38 I'll get off at the next stop. 我下一站要下車。

39 ① I'll get off here.
② I'm getting off. 我要在這裡下車。

40 Ⓐ Am I on the bus to Chinatown?

Ⓑ ① Yes, you are.
② No, you aren't. You should get off at the next stop.

Ⓐ 這班車有到中國城嗎？

Ⓑ ① 有。
② 沒有耶，你得在下一站下車。

41 Ⓐ How many stops to Central Park?

Ⓑ It's the seventh stop.

Ⓐ 中央公園是第幾站？

Ⓑ 是第七站。

3 搭地下鐵 🎧 62

42 Where is the nearest subway station?
最近的地鐵車站在哪裡？

43 May I have a subway route map?
我可以拿一份地鐵的路線圖嗎？

44 What line should I take to go to Central Park?
去中央公園要搭哪一條線呢？

45 Where do I change trains to go to Wall Street?
去華爾街要在哪裡轉車呢？

46 Where can I get a subway token?
哪裡可以買到地鐵用的代幣？

47 Where is a ticket machine? 車票的自動販賣機在哪裡？

48 How much is one token?
一枚代幣（乘車專用硬幣）多少錢？

49 Ten tokens, please. 要十枚代幣。

50 Can I have two packs of tokens? 我要兩包代幣。

51 Does this train stop at Times Square?
這地鐵有停時代廣場嗎？

52 Which exit should I take for City Hall?
往市政府的出口是哪一個？

53 Where is the exit? 出口在哪裡？

4 搭電車或長程列車

54 I'd like to see a timetable. 我想看時刻表。

55 Can I buy a ticket on the train? 可以在車內買票嗎？

56 A one-way ticket to Chicago, please.
我要一張到芝加哥的單程票。

57 Two round-trip tickets to Boston, please.
我要兩張到波士頓的來回票。

58 Tickets for two adults to London, please.
我要兩張到倫敦的全票。

59 Two tickets for the 2:30 express. 兩點三十分的快車票兩張。

60 How much is the fare to Chicago? 到芝加哥要多少錢？

61 What's the round-trip fare? 來回票多少錢？

62 What's the express charge? 快車票多少錢？

63 What's the sleeper fare? 臥舖車票多少錢？

64 Do I have to make a reservation for a limited express train?
特快車需要先訂位嗎？

65 I'd like to reserve a seat to Chicago. 我要訂往芝加哥的票。

66 I'd like the lower berth. 我要下舖。〔上舖是upper berth〕

67 Does the train have a dining car? 這輛車上有餐車嗎？

68 Is this the right platform for the train to Chicago?
往芝加哥的車在這個月台搭嗎？

69 Which platform should I use to take the A train?
A車在哪個月台？

70 Which track does the train to Las Vegas leave from?
哪一路火車是要去拉斯維加斯的？

71 How many train stops to San Diego? 聖地牙哥是第幾站？

72 Is this the local or express train? 這列是普通車，還是快車？

73 Does the express train stop at Osaka? 這列快車有停大阪嗎？

74 How long does it take to get to Boston? 到波士頓要多久時間？

75 What time does this train get to L.A.? 這班車幾點到洛杉磯？

76 Where are the reserved seats? 訂位的位子在哪裡？

77 I took the wrong train. At which station should I get off?
我搭錯車了，要在哪一站下車才好呢？

78 At which station should I change trains?
我應該在哪一站轉車呢？

在國外旅遊時，如果想要看遍景點、又想玩得划算，那交通工具的使用就很重要。在許多大城市都可買一張票，就能搭乘地鐵、公車甚至遊輪；有時也有搭乘交通工具可免費參觀博物館或著名景點的套票。出國前先上網查詢或是向旅行社詢問，不但可省下一筆費用，還可看到更多景點！

搭火車旅遊是非常方便又容易的事，在歐洲大陸更為便利，可以在事前向各大旅行社購買。其中分為許多不同的票種，例如：

Eurail Pass（歐洲十七國聯營火車票）
ScanRail Pass（北歐四國聯營火車票）
Balkan Flexipass（巴爾幹半島彈性火車票）

在北美旅遊時，也有方便的火車系統可搭：

North America Rail Pass（北美聯營火車票，同時遊覽美國及加拿大）
National Rail Pass（美國火車聯票，可遊遍全美）
Northeast Rail Pass（美國東北部火車聯票，限於美國東北部）
Far West Rail Pass（美西火車聯票，限於美西）

以車程距離來區分，市區公車稱為 bus，若是長途客運，在美國稱 long-distance bus，在英國則稱 coach。

以公車的外型來區分，巴士可分為單層巴士或雙層巴士（double-decker）。雙層巴士是英國的「特產」，許多人到英國時，都會嚐嚐搭乘雙層巴士的滋味。

以功能來區分，除了一般的公車外，許多的大城市都有觀光巴士（tour bus）。觀光巴士有時也會與其他大眾運輸工具配合，買了票後，除了可以在限定的日期內自由上下車參觀名勝古蹟、著名觀光景點外，還可以搭乘其他交通工具，非常方便。

在美國，市區公車都是投幣式，車上不找零，所以上車前記得先準備一些零錢。如果是要轉乘其他巴士，司機會給一張轉乘卡（transfer card），這樣下段旅程將可較便宜或是免費。

在英國則相反，上車購票時司機會找零，有時可以在上車時就告知是買來回票，相對會較便宜且方便，回程上車時出示票券即可。至於長途巴士，則大多是先在站內購票後再上車。

10

DIALOGUE

Ⓐ I'd like to rent a car.

Ⓑ What kind of car would you like?

Ⓐ Something that is medium-sized and gets good mileage.

Ⓑ Would you prefer a Japanese car?

Ⓐ Something in the 2-liter class that is easy to drive and has left-hand steering.

Ⓑ Why don't you try that model over there?
   May I see your driver's license and credit card?

Ⓐ 我要租輛車。

Ⓑ 您要租什麼樣的車呢?

Ⓐ 我想租比較省油的中型車。

Ⓑ 您喜歡開日本車嗎?

Ⓐ 只要好開就好,我要左駕的車,排氣量約2000c.c.左右。

Ⓑ 那您可以試試那輛車,我可以看一下您的駕照和信用卡嗎?

rent a car	租車	rent 是指要付費的出租
medium-sized	中型的	也可以說 middle-sized 「小型的」是 small-sized 「大型的」是 large-sized
get good mileage	省油	也可以用形容詞 economical
left-hand steering	左邊方向盤	「左駕的車」有以下兩種說法： ① a left-hand-drive car ② a car with left-hand drive

有些國家幅員遼闊，因此在交通不方便的地區，出門就得仰賴車子。如果你要去較偏僻的地方觀光，那最好在國內辦好國際駕照和租車手續，這樣到了當地拿車才比較方便。

如果要在當地租車，可以在機場的觀光服務中心、租車櫃檯或是在飯店辦理手續。辦理時需要出示護照、國際駕照和信用卡。另外，為了以防萬一，最好投保。

1 IDP (International Driving Permit) 國際駕照

2 car insurance 汽車險

3 rental agreement 租約

4 rental charge 租金

5 deposit 保證金

6 no-show fee 違約金

7 mileage 哩程數

8 gas station 加油站

9 gas pump 油泵

10 gas pump nozzle 油槍

11 regular gasoline 普通汽油

12 plus gasoline 次高級汽油

13 premium gasoline 高級汽油

14 diesel fuel 柴油

15 unleaded gasoline 無鉛汽油

16 broken down 拋錨

17 flat tire 爆胎

18 under construction 道路施工

19 parking lot 停車場

20 parking space 停車位

21 parking meter
停車計費表

22 road map 交通路線圖

23 traffic sign; road sign 交通標誌

EXIT 6

ROAD SIGNS
道路交通標誌
NEXT EXIT
下一個出口

10
VOCABULARY
租車

改道行駛

停車拖吊

全日禁止停車

讓路

前方道路施工

禁止進入

限速 55 哩

道路錯誤

95 號州際公路
（美國）

66 號公路
（美國）

此路不通

單行道

Useful Expressions

1 找租車公司

❶ Where can I rent a car? 我在哪裡可以租到車子呢？

❷ Are there any car rental companies around here?
這附近有租車公司嗎？

❸ Where's the nearest rent-a-car company?
最近的租車公司在哪裡？

❹ I want to rent a car, but how do I go about it?
我想要租車，我應該如何辦理呢？

2 到租車公司租車

❺ I made a reservation in Taiwan. My name is Amy Lee.
我叫李愛咪，我在台灣已經預約好了。

❻ I have a reservation. My name is Ginny Lin.
我有預租，我叫林靜妮。

❼ I'd like to rent a car. 我要租輛車。

❽ Do you have one available now? 現在有車子可以租用嗎？

❾ May I see a price list? 我可以看一下價目表嗎？

❿ Can I see your rent-a-car list?
我可以看一下出租車輛的清單嗎？

11 ① What type of a car would you like?
② What model do you want?
您想租哪一種款式的車？

12 What kind of cars do you have? 有哪幾種車款呢？

13 I'd like one that gets good gas mileage.
我想要較省油的車。

14 Do you have Japanese cars? 有日本車嗎？

15 Do you have any sports cars? 有跑車嗎？

16 An automatic sedan, please. 我想要租一輛自排的轎車。

17 I'd like a compact car. 我要一輛小型車。

18 I'd like a small van. 我想要租一輛小型箱型車。

19 I'd like an SUV. 想要租一輛休旅車。〔SUV = sport-utility vehicle〕

compact 小型車

van 箱型車

SUV 休旅車

sports car 跑車

20 I'd like one with an automatic transmission.
我想要租一輛自排車。

21 I prefer a manual transmission.
我想要租手排車。

22 How many days do you want to rent this car?
這輛車你要租多久？

manual car
手排車

automatic car
自排車

23 I'd like to rent it for one day. 我想要租一天。

24 I'd like to rent this type of car for a week.
這種車款我想要租一個星期。

25 ① Can I leave it at my destination?
② Can I drop it off at my destination?
可以在我要去的地方還車嗎？

26 I'd like to rent a car for a one-way trip only.
我想租可以在目的地還車的車子。

27 Can I leave the car at any rental office in the country?
我可以在這個國家內的任何地方還車嗎？

28 What's the drop-off charge? 中途還車的費用是多少？

29 When do I have to return the car? 最遲是什麼時候要還車？

30 Where do I return the car? 我要在哪裡還車？

3 詢問費用及保險 🎧 68

31 ① What is the rate?
　　② How much does it cost? 租車費用是多少錢？

32 I'll pay by credit card. 我用信用卡付帳。

33 Is the mileage free? 沒有限制行駛哩數嗎？

34 ① Does it include gas?
　　② Is the cost of gas included in that? 有含油費嗎？

35 ① Do I have to pay a deposit?
　　② Do you need a deposit? 需要付訂金嗎？

36 Does the price include insurance? 這個費用有含保險嗎？

37 Is the insurance charge separate? 保險費另外算嗎？

38 ① I'd like to insure it.
　　② I'd like to buy insurance. 我想要買保險。

39 I'd like full insurance. 我想要買全險。

40 Am I fully covered in case of an accident?
發生事故時，保險公司會全部給付嗎？

41 What's the extra charge if I don't return it on time?
如果車子沒有準時歸還的話，那逾期的費用要怎麼算呢？

42 How much will it be if I go over the rental period?
如果超過歸還日期，要加付多少錢呢？

4 在加油站

43 Is there a gas station around here? 這附近有加油站嗎？

44 My car is out of gas. 我的車沒油了。

45 Fill it up, please. 請加滿。

46 Fill it up with regular, please. 普通汽油，請加滿。

47 Ten dollars of gas, please. 麻煩加十塊美金的汽油。

48 Five gallons of gas, please. 麻煩加五加侖的汽油。

49 How much is it per gallon? 一加侖的汽油是多少錢？

50 Please show me how to fill the gas tank. 請教我怎麼加油。

51 How do I use this pump? 這個油槍要怎麼使用呢？

52 Check the battery, please. 請幫我檢查電瓶。

53 Charge the battery, please. 請幫我把電瓶充電。

54 Check the brakes, please. 請幫我檢查煞車。

55 Check the tires, please. 請幫我檢查輪胎。

56 Wash the car, please. 請幫我洗車。

57 Clean the windshield, please. 請幫我清潔雨刷。

58 My car has broken down. 我的車故障了。

59 This car isn't in good condition. 這輛車的狀況不太好。

60 It makes a strange noise. 它會發出奇怪的聲音。

61 I've got a flat. 我的車爆胎了。

62 The engine won't start. 引擎無法發動。

child seat 兒童座椅

steering wheel 方向盤

**manual brake;
parking brake** 手煞車

gauge 儀表板

horn 喇叭

gear 排檔桿

engine 引擎

battery 電瓶

**GPS (Global Positioning
System)** 導航系統

11

問路

ASKING FOR DIRECTIONS

DIALOGUE

Ⓐ Excuse me. Can you tell me the way to the Hilton Hotel?

Ⓑ Go straight down this street about five blocks, and you'll see a drugstore on the corner. When you get there, turn right. You'll see it just on your left.

Ⓐ How long will it take me to get there on foot?

Ⓑ About 7 minutes.

Ⓐ I see. Thanks for your help.

Ⓐ 不好意思,請問希爾頓飯店要怎麼走?

Ⓑ 這條馬路直走大約五條街左右,轉角處有間藥房,看到藥房後右轉,右轉後的左手邊就可以看到了。

Ⓐ 從這裡走過去要多久?

Ⓑ 大概7分鐘左右。

Ⓐ 哦,那我知道了,謝謝你。

Study Points

Can you tell me the way to . . .?	請問去……要怎麼走？	較客氣的問路說法
Go straight down . . .	往……一直走	在美國，道路的單位都是用 block
turn right	右轉	也可以說成：turn to the right
just on your left	就在你的左手邊	介系詞要用 on
Thanks for your help.	謝謝您的幫助。	記得要禮貌地感謝對方

若在國外迷了路，請不要害怕，鼓起勇氣向陌生人問個路吧！問路時，可以這麼說：

■ Excuse me. Can you tell me how to get to . . .?

不好意思，請問一下，
到……要怎麼走呢？

■ Excuse me. Do you know where the . . . is?

不好意思，請問一下，
……在哪裡呢？

另外，要如何選對人來問路也是很重要的，最好是挑那種看起來不是在趕路的人，也就是走路不會走得很快的人。對於太親切的人，人們容易喪失警覺心，因此很可能會上當受騙，所以這個也要特別小心。最後問完路，別忘了向對方說聲「Thank you.」喔！

1 lose one's way 迷路

2 landmark 地標

3 direction 方向

4 block 街區

5 cross the street 穿越馬路

6 pass the station 路過車站

7 at the intersection 在十字路口

8 at the corner 在轉角

9 on your left 在你的左手邊

10 on your right 在你的右手邊

11 turn left 左轉 **12** turn right 右轉

13 go straight 直走

1 迷路時 🎧72

❶ Excuse me. I think I've lost my way. Where am I now?
不好意思，我迷路了。請問這裡是哪裡？

❷ I'm a stranger here. 我第一次來這裡。

❸ I'm not familiar with this area. 這附近我不熟。

❹ Where am I now on this map?
我現在在這張地圖上的哪個位置？

❺ Please show me where I am on this map.
可以請你比給我看我現在在地圖上的哪個地方嗎？

❻ Where does this street lead to? 這條路通往哪裡？

❼ What's the name of this street? 這條街的街名是什麼？

❽ What street is this? 這是哪一條街？

❾ Which way is north? 哪邊是北邊？

❿ What part of the city is this? 這裡是位於市區的哪一邊？

⓫ Do you have any idea where this address is?
你知道這個住址在哪裡嗎？

⓬ How do I get to this address [place]?
要怎麼去這個住址〔地方〕呢？

2 詢問路線 🎧73

⑬ Where is the bus stop, please?
請問公車站在哪裡呢？

⑭ Where is the nearest station?
最近的車站在哪裡？

⑮ Can you show me the way to the nearest subway station?
請問最近的地鐵站要怎麼走呢？

⑯ How do I get to Hyde Park? 請問去海德公園要怎麼走？

⑰ Can you tell me how to get to the zoo?
請問動物園要怎麼去？

⑱ Do you know the way to the Hilton Hotel?
請問去希爾頓飯店要怎麼走？

⑲ Where is the Central Bank? 中央銀行在哪裡呢？

⑳ Is this the right way to the British Museum?
去大英博物館走這條路對嗎？

㉑ What's the shortcut to Plaza Hollywood?
去好萊塢廣場的捷徑是什麼？

㉒ On which side of the street? 在馬路的哪一邊呢？

㉓ Is it correct to go straight? 一直直走就是了嗎？

24 Are there any landmarks along the way?
沿路上有什麼明顯地標嗎？

25 ① You won't miss it.
② You can't miss it. 那很好找的。

26
Ⓐ How long will it take on foot?
Ⓑ It's about a 10-minute walk from here.
Ⓐ 走路的話，要走多久？
Ⓑ 從這裡大概要走十分鐘的路程。

27
Ⓐ How far is it from here?
Ⓑ About 500 meters.
Ⓐ 離這裡有多遠的距離？
Ⓑ 大概五百公尺。

28
Ⓐ Is it (very) far from here?
Ⓑ No, it's not that far.
Ⓐ 離這裡（很）遠嗎？
Ⓑ 不會啦，不會太遠。

29 ① Can I walk there?
② Can I get there on foot? 走路可以到嗎？

30 ① You should take a bus.
② You should go by bus. 你還是搭公車去比較好。

31 Which direction is 42nd Street? 第42條街是哪個方向？

W.C.（原指 water closet，比較少用）

3 詢問洗手間

32 Excuse me. Where can I find a restroom?
請問洗手間在哪裡？

33 Excuse me. Do you have a restroom? 請問有洗手間嗎？

34 Is there a restroom nearby? 這附近有洗手間嗎？

35 Where is the restroom? 哪裡有洗手間呢？

36 Where is the nearest restroom? 最近的洗手間在哪裡呢？

37 May I use your restroom? 可以借個洗手間嗎？

38 Where's the men's room? 男廁在哪裡？

39 Where's the ladies' room? 女廁在哪裡？

40 It is occupied. 有人在用。

41 It is vacant. 沒有人在用。

12

DIALOGUE

Ⓐ Do you have any sightseeing tours of the city?

Ⓑ We have half-day tours, full-day tours, and nighttime tours available.

Ⓐ Which tour includes more famous places?

Ⓑ You'd probably like the full-day tour the best. Niagara Falls is included in the itinerary.

Ⓐ Does the tour include a guide?

Ⓑ Yes, we have a Chinese-speaking guide.

Ⓐ 有沒有市區的觀光行程？

Ⓑ 有半日遊、一日遊和夜間觀光等行程。

Ⓐ 哪個團的知名景點比較多？

Ⓑ 那你可能會比較喜歡一日遊，這個行程有包含去尼加拉瓜大瀑布。

Ⓐ 那個行程會有導遊跟著嗎？

Ⓑ 有的，有會説中文的導遊。

Study Points

sightseeing tour	觀光團	sightseer 是「觀光客」
half-day tours, full-day tours, and nighttime tours	半日遊、一日遊和夜間行程	nighttime 是「夜間的」
available	可得到的	available 的發音是 [əˋveləbḷ]
itinerary	旅遊行程	itinerary 的發音是 [aɪˋtɪnəˏrɛrɪ]
a tour include a guide	含導遊同行的行程	guide 是「導遊」

雖然在出國觀光之前，可以從許多的情報雜誌或觀光旅遊的書籍中獲取許多資訊，但實際去參觀的時候就不見得像書上寫的那樣了。

這時候你可以去當地的**遊客中心**（tourist information），索取最新情報。想要有不一樣的玩法，只要好好地利用旅客服務中心，就可以挖到很多寶貴的資料喔。

1 travel agency 旅行社

2 tourist information 遊客中心

3 tourist 遊客

4 tour group 旅遊團

5 tour guide 導遊

6 sightseeing bus 觀光巴士

7 **itinerary** 旅遊行程

8 **guidebook** 旅遊指南

9 **spot** 景點

10 **gift shop** 禮品店

11 **take pictures** 拍照

12 **photograph** 相片

1 遊客中心 (77)

1 Can you tell me where the tourist information office is?
請問旅客服務中心在哪裡？

2 Do you have a city map? 這裡有市區地圖嗎？

3 Do you have a free map of this area?
有沒有可以免費索取的當地地圖呢？

4 I'd like a bus route map. 我想要一張公車路線圖。

5 Where can I get a New York Subway map?
在哪裡可以拿到紐約地鐵的路線圖呢？

6 Are there any tour guidebooks? 有沒有觀光的旅遊指南呢？

7 Do you have a brochure for sightseeing?
有觀光手冊嗎？

2 詢問觀光行程

8 I'd like to see the sights of the city. 我想要做市區觀光。

9 Do you have any sightseeing tours of the city?
有市區觀光團嗎？

10 I'd like to take a sightseeing tour. 我想報名參加觀光團。

11 What kind of tours do you have? 有哪些行程呢？

12 Can you recommend some popular tours?
可以推薦一些比較受歡迎的行程給我嗎？

13 Do you have a full-day tour?
有沒有一日遊的團呢？

14 What kind of sightseeing bus tours do you have?
有哪些觀光巴士的團呢？

15 Do you have any half-day sightseeing bus tours?
有沒有半天的觀光巴士團呢？

16 I'd like to sign up for the Niagara Falls tour.
我想報名參加尼加拉瓜大瀑布的旅遊團。

17 Which tour is best for seeing museums?
要參觀博物館的話，選哪個行程最好？

18 Is there a tour that includes a Broadway show?
有沒有可以看百老匯的團呢？

19 Do you have any tours of the islands? 有環島的旅行團嗎？

3 詢問旅遊團細節

20 Would you please give me some details about the tour?
可以告訴我這個行程的一些詳細內容嗎？

21 Is it a half-day tour? 那是半天的行程嗎？

22 What can I see on the tour? 那個團是參觀什麼的呢？

23 Does it include a visit to Disneyland?
那個團有去迪士尼樂園嗎？

24 How long is the tour? 這個團要去多久？

25 Is lunch included in the tour? 有包含午餐嗎？

26 What is the charge? 費用是多少呢？

27 Does the charge include meals? 有含伙食費嗎？

28 I'd prefer something less expensive than this tour.
我要找的是比這個還便宜的團。

29 What is the difference between this tour and the more
expensive ones? 價錢高的團和價錢低的團，有什麼不一樣呢？

30 Where will we have lunch? 中午是在哪裡用餐呢？

31 Where do we get on the bus? 在哪裡搭巴士呢？

32 What time does the tour start? 幾點出發呢？

33 When and from where does it leave? 幾點在哪裡出發呢？

34 What time and where should we wait?
幾點在哪裡等比較好呢？

35 Will we have any free time during the tour?
在行程中有自由時間嗎？

36 Do you have a Chinese-speaking guide?
有會説中文的導遊一起去嗎？

37 Does the guide speak any languages other than English?
導遊只會説英文嗎？

Ticket Sales
售票處

Historic Building
古蹟建築

Cinema
電影院

Café
咖啡廳

Museum
博物館

Photography
照相服務

Beach
海灘

Restaurant
餐廳

4 觀光景點 🎧 80

38 What time does this museum open?
這間博物館是幾點開門？

39 How much is the admission fee? 門票是多少錢？

40 Two adults and three children, please.
麻煩給我兩張全票和三張兒童票。

41 One student ticket, please. 請給我一張學生票。

42 Can I take pictures inside the museum?
博物館裡面可以照相嗎？

43 May I take a picture of this building?
我可以拍這棟建築物嗎？

44 Is this the correct way? 往這邊走沒錯吧？

45 Where is the entrance? 入口在哪裡？

46 What's that structure [building]? 那棟建築物是什麼？

47 Can I go into this building? 可以進去這棟建築物裡面嗎？

48 When was it built? 它是什麼時候建造的？

49 How old is it? 它有多久歷史了？

50 What's it famous for? 它是以什麼聞名的呢？

51 Where is the gift shop? 哪裡有禮品店呢？

52 What time shall we meet next? 下次的集合時間是幾點？

53 What time should I be back? 在幾點之前一定要回來集合呢？

5 拍照

54 May I take pictures here? 這裡可以拍照嗎？

55 Would you take a picture for me? 可以請你幫我照張相嗎？

56 Can you please take a picture of us?
不好意思，可以請你幫我們拍照嗎？

57 Just press this button. 只要按下這個鈕就行了。

58 Take a picture with that building in the background, please. 請以那棟建築物為背景，幫我們拍照。

59 Please push the button after the red light comes on.
等紅色的燈亮了之後，再按鈕。

60 One more, please. 麻煩再照一張。

61 Excuse me. May I take your picture, please?
抱歉，可以讓我拍您嗎？

62 Excuse me. Could I please take a picture with you?
我可以跟您一起拍照嗎？

63 Would you pose with me? 你可以跟我合照嗎？

13

生病

SICKNESS

DIALOGUE

ⓐ What's the matter?

ⓑ I have a slight fever, and I also have pain on the right side of my chest when I cough.

ⓐ Where does it hurt?

ⓑ Right in this area. I am having difficulty breathing.

ⓐ Let's check your chest. Take a deep breath. Let it out slowly. How do you feel now?

ⓑ I feel better now.

ⓐ OK, there is nothing to worry about. Maybe it was caused by fatigue from the long journey.

ⓐ 你怎麼了?

ⓑ 我有點發燒,而且只要一咳嗽,右邊的胸口就會疼痛。

ⓐ 是哪裡痛?

ⓑ 會痛這邊,然後會覺得呼吸困難。

ⓐ 那我來檢查一下你的胸部。深呼吸,把氣慢慢地吐出來。你現在覺得怎麼樣?

ⓑ 我覺得好多了。

ⓐ 這大概是長程旅行所引起的疲勞,不用擔心。

Study Points

I have a . . .	我有……（症狀）	跟醫生說明自己症狀時的表達方式
have difficulty breathing	呼吸困難	「have difficulty . . .」表示對某事有困難
take a deep breath	深呼吸	動詞要用 take
feel better	感覺好些	用來表達身體感覺好一點
nothing to worry about	不用擔心	用來表達身體沒有大礙

出外旅行時，為了預防在國外生病，盡可能不要飲用生水，或是玩得過頭。萬一不小心生病了，也是要去看醫生喔！

歐美貫徹醫藥分級制度，所以除了阿斯匹靈、止瀉藥和一般外傷的藥之外，如果沒有醫師的處方箋，無法輕易在藥局買到其他的藥物。而且，歐美的醫療機構大都是採預約制，所以生病時要先用電話預約看病，如果情況很危急，可以到大醫院的急診處就醫。

在美國，警察、消防隊和救護車的緊急電話號碼都是911。接通救護車的電話時，可以說：

- **Ambulance, please.**
  我要叫救護車。

ambulance 救護車

fire truck 消防車

tow truck 拖吊車

police car 警車

1 hospital 綜合醫院

2 clinic 診所

3 pharmacy; drugstore 藥房

4 first-aid kit 急救箱

5 symptom 症狀

6 checkup 檢查

7 prescription 處方箋

8 injection 打針

9 medicine 藥

10 flu 流行性感冒

11 cold 感冒

12 indigestion 消化不良

13 stomachache
胃痛

14 food poisoning
食物中毒

15 toothache 牙齒痛

16 allergy 過敏

17 Band-Aid
OK 繃

18 trauma 外傷

DIFFERENT KINDS OF PAIN
疼痛種類

1	acute pain	急性疼痛
2	sudden pain	突然痛起來
3	chronic pain	慢性疼痛
4	sharp pain	刺痛
5	dull pain	隱隱作痛
6	severe pain	極度疼痛
7	stinging pain	刺痛
8	throbbing pain	抽痛
9	gripping pain	絞痛
10	splitting pain	割傷的痛
11	continuous pain	連續不斷的痛

DISEASE
疾病名稱

1	high blood pressure	高血壓
2	diabetes	糖尿病
3	heart disease	心臟病
4	heart attack	心臟病發
5	asthma	氣喘
6	cancer	癌症
7	gout	痛風
8	depression	憂鬱症

HOSPITAL UNITS
醫院單位

Registration Office	掛號處
Emergency Room	急診室
First Aid Station	急救站
Appointments	預約門診
Waiting Room	候診室
Consultation Room	診室
Medication and Injection	吃藥及注射室
Cashier	批價處
Dispensary	領藥處
Pharmacy	藥局
Diagnosis Certificates	診斷證明書
Outpatient Department	門診部
Inpatient Department	住院部
Admission Information	住院服務中心
Discharge	出院處
Intensive Care Unit	加護病房
Ward	病房
Operation Room (OR)	手術室
Family Lounge	家屬休息室
Patient Beds Only	病床專用電梯
Mortuary	太平間

Department	
Medical Department	內科
Surgical Department	外科
Pediatrics Department	小兒科
Obstetrics and Gynecology Department	婦產科
Ophthalmology Department	眼科
Dental Department	牙科
ENT (Ear-Nose-Throat) Department	耳鼻喉科
Urology Department	泌尿科
Dermatology Department	皮膚科
Orthopedic Surgery Department	矯形外科
Trauma Department	創傷外科
Plastic Surgery	整形外科
Cardiology Department	心臟病科
Psychiatry Department	精神病科
Orthopedics Department	骨科
Neurology Department	神經科

HUMAN BODY (I)
人體部位

- Brain 大腦
- Larynx 喉頭
- Esophagus 食道
- Heart 心臟
- Liver 肝臟
- Lungs 肺臟
- Stomach 胃
- Gallbladder 膽囊
- Spleen 脾臟
- Pancreas 胰臟
- Kidneys 腎臟
- Large Intestine 大腸
- Small Intestine 小腸
- Appendix 盲腸
- Urinary Bladder 膀胱

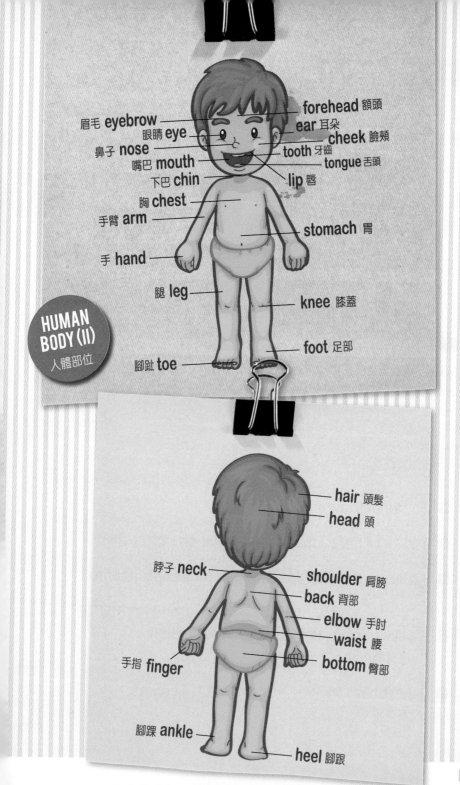

HUMAN BODY (II)
人體部位

眉毛 eyebrow
眼睛 eye
鼻子 nose
嘴巴 mouth
下巴 chin
胸 chest
手臂 arm
手 hand
腿 leg
腳趾 toe

forehead 額頭
ear 耳朵
cheek 臉頰
tooth 牙齒
tongue 舌頭
lip 唇
stomach 胃
knee 膝蓋
foot 足部

hair 頭髮
head 頭

脖子 neck
shoulder 肩膀
back 背部
elbow 手肘
waist 腰
手指 finger
bottom 臀部

腳踝 ankle
heel 腳跟

make an appointment
預約醫生

take one's temperature
量體溫

take one's blood pressure
量血壓

1 在醫院窗口 84

1 I'd like to see a doctor. 我想要看病。

---

2 I'd like to have a medical examination. 我想做個檢查。

---

3 I'd like to make an appointment for a consultation.
我想預約看病。

---

4 I'd like to be examined as soon as possible.
（沒有預約時）我想快一點看病。

---

5 I don't have an appointment, but it's urgent.
我沒有預約，可是我很急。

常見的
感冒症狀

fever 發燒

headache 頭痛

sore throat 喉嚨痛

cough 咳嗽

runny nose 流鼻水

stuffy nose 鼻塞

sneeze 打噴嚏

2 身體症狀

6 I have a slight fever. 我有點發燒。

7 I feel feverish. 我可能發燒了。

8 I have a 39.5 degree Centigrade fever.
我燒到39.5度。

9 My temperature rose suddenly. 我突然發高燒。

10 I've had a high temperature for some time now.
我一直高燒不退。

11 I feel chilly. 我覺得全身發冷。

12 I'm afraid I've caught a cold. 我好像感冒了。

13 ① I have a slight cold.
② I've caught a bit of a cold. 我得了輕微的感冒。

14 I've got a head cold. 我感冒了。

15 I can't get rid of this cold. 我感冒一直沒有好。

16 I feel languid. 我覺得渾身無力。

17 I feel dizzy when I stand up. 我站起來就覺得頭昏眼花。

18 I don't feel well. 我不太舒服。

19 I feel very sick. 我覺得很不舒服。

20 I cannot sleep. 我睡不著。

21 I feel dizzy. 我覺得頭暈。

22 ① I feel like vomiting.
② I feel like throwing up. 我想吐。

23 I vomited last night. 我昨晚吐了。

24 I can't keep any food down. 我不管吃什麼都會吐。

25 ① I don't have an appetite.
② I don't feel like eating. 我沒有食欲。

26 I have high blood pressure. 我有高血壓。

27 I can't stop sneezing. 我一直打噴嚏。

28 I can't stop coughing. 我一直咳嗽。

3 頭、臉、脖子等症狀

29 I have a headache. 我頭痛。

30 My head is throbbing. 我覺得頭陣陣抽痛。

31 I have a splitting headache. 我覺得頭痛得要裂開了。

32 I feel heavy in the head. 我覺得頭暈。

33 I have a migraine. 我有偏頭痛。

34 I have a crick in my neck. 我脖子痙攣。

35 I strained my neck. 我的脖子扭到了。

4 嘴、喉嚨、牙齒等症狀

36 My mouth is rough. 我的嘴巴破了。

37 I have inflammation in my mouth. 我的嘴巴發炎了。

38 My mouth is swollen. 我的嘴巴腫起來。

39 I have a sore throat. 我喉嚨痛。

40 I have swollen tonsils. 我扁桃腺發炎。

41 I have a toothache. 我牙痛。

42 My teeth feel unduly sensitive. 我的牙齒對冷熱很敏感。

43 My decayed tooth aches. 我的蛀牙在痛。

5 鼻、眼、耳等症狀

44 There is swelling in my nose. 我鼻子裡面腫起來了。

45 I have a stuffed nose. 我鼻塞。

46 My nose is runny. 我流鼻水。

47 My eyes hurt. 我眼睛痛。

48 My right eye is swollen. 我右邊的眼睛腫起來了。

49 There is a ringing in my ears. 我覺得耳鳴。

50 I have a severe earache. 我耳朵很痛。

6 胸部和腹部的症狀

51 I have heart trouble. 我有心臟病的問題。

52 I suffer from asthma. 我有氣喘。

53 My chest hurts. 我覺得胸口難受。

54 I've got a pain in my chest. 我胸口痛。

55 I feel choked up. 我覺得呼吸困難。

56 My chest hurts when I breathe. 我一呼吸，胸口就會痛。

57 I have a stomachache. 我胃痛。

58 I have abdominal pain on my left side. 我左側腹痛。

59 My stomach burns. 我胃在灼痛。

60 I have heartburn. 我覺得胃灼熱。

61 My stomach aches after I eat a meal. 我吃完飯後胃就在痛。

62 I have a gripping pain in my stomach. 我胃絞痛。

63 I feel as if I have a bulging, stuffed stomach. 我覺得胃很脹。

64 I have a heavy stomach. 我胃消化不良。

65 I have an upset stomach. 我拉肚子。

66 I have loose bowels. 我拉肚子。

67 I have had no bowel movement for three days.
我有三天沒排便了。

68 I suffer from constipation. 我有便秘。

69 I have terrible menstrual pain. 我生理痛，痛得很厲害。

vomit 嘔吐

fart 放屁

diarrhea 拉肚子

constipation 便秘

7 手腳、背部、腰、肩、關節等症狀

70
　① I have a pain in my back.
　② I have a backache. 我的背會痛。

71　I suffer from terrible back pain. 我的背痛得很厲害。

72　My joints ache. 我關節痛。

73　I've strained my back. 我的背閃到了。

74　I often have cramps when sleeping.
　　我睡覺的時候常會抽筋。

75　I have terribly stiff shoulders. 我的肩膀很僵硬。

8 過敏與外傷 　91

76　I have severe hives. 我的蕁麻疹很嚴重。

77　I feel itchy all over my body. 我覺得全身發癢。

78　I'm allergic to antibiotics. 我對抗生素過敏。

79　I'm injured. 我受傷了。

80　I'm badly hurt. 我傷得很嚴重。

81　I've broken my leg. 我摔斷腿了。

82　I think I twisted my foot. 我的腳好像扭傷了。

swelling 腫脹　　bruise 青腫　　fracture 骨折

sprain 扭傷

bleeding 流血

---

83 My shoulder is badly bruised. 我肩膀擦傷得很嚴重。

---

84 I'm afraid I have dislocated my left arm.
我的左手好像脫臼了。

---

85 I burned my finger. 我的手指燙傷了。

---

86 It's bleeding. 流血了。

---

9 醫生對病患說的話　

87　① Is something bothering you?
　　② What seems to be the trouble? 你哪裡不舒服了嗎？

---

physician 內科醫生　　surgeon 外科醫生　　dentist 牙醫

88 **What kind of pain are you having?** 怎麼個痛法？

89 **How long have you had this pain?** 你從什麼時候開始痛的？

90 **Point to where it hurts.** 你哪邊痛，請用手指指給我看。

91 **Do you have an appetite?** 你食欲好嗎？

92 **What did you eat yesterday?** 你昨天吃了什麼東西？

93 **Do you have diarrhea?** 你有拉肚子嗎？

94 **Did you have a bowel movement this morning?**
你今天早上有排便嗎？

95 **Have you been sleeping well?** 你最近睡得好嗎？

96 **Let's take a look.** 讓我來檢查看看。

97 **Let's take your temperature.** 量一下你的體溫。

98 **Let's take your blood pressure.** 量一下你的血壓。

99 **Let's take your pulse.** 量一下你的脈搏。

100 I want you to have an x-ray. 你要去照張X光。

101 Do you have any allergies? 你會過敏嗎？

102 Do you have any other medical conditions?
你有什麼其他的疾病嗎？

103 Roll up your sleeve. 把你的袖子捲起來。

104 Take off your shirt, please. 請把你的襯衫脫下來。

105 Unbutton your shirt, please. 請解開襯衫的鈕扣。

106 Open your mouth wide and say "Ah."
把你的嘴巴張大一點，說聲「啊」。

107 Take a deep breath. 深呼吸。

108 Lie down here. 躺在這裡。

109 Breathe out . . . in . . . 吐氣……，吸氣……

110 Breathe in slowly. 慢慢吸氣。

111 You shouldn't eat greasy foods. 你要避免吃太油的食物。

112 You shouldn't drink too much alcohol.
你要避免喝太多含有酒精的飲料。

113 You shouldn't drink any alcohol.
你不可以喝任何含酒精的飲料。

114 Please stop smoking and drinking. 不可以吸菸或喝酒。

115 Please see a doctor tomorrow. 請明天再來複診。

116　Please see a doctor if the symptom worsens.
如果症狀變嚴重了，你就要再去看醫生。

117　I'll write a prescription for you. 我會開藥方給你。

118　I'll give you a prescription, and you can have it filled at a drugstore. 我會開處方箋給你，請拿到藥局配藥。

119　Take this prescription to a pharmacy. You can get the medicine there. 請拿著這張處方箋到藥局拿藥。

10 到藥局買藥　🎧93

120　Is there a pharmacy nearby? 這附近有藥局嗎？

121　Here is my prescription. 這是我的處方箋。

122　Can I get my prescription filled here?
可以在這裡請你配藥嗎？

123　Please fill this prescription. 請幫我配這張處方箋的藥。

124　Would you fill this prescription, please?
請照這張處方箋配藥。

125　　Ⓐ　Do I need a prescription to buy this?
　　　Ⓑ　These tablets are available over-the-counter.
　　　Ⓐ　要有處方箋才可以買到這個藥嗎？
　　　Ⓑ　這些藥片沒有處方箋也可以買。

126 I need some medicine. 請給我一些藥。

127 Do you have stomach medicine? 有胃藥嗎？

128 I need something to help me sleep.
我需要一些可以幫助睡眠的藥。

129 I want medicine for a cold. 我需要感冒藥。

130 ① Does it have any side effects?
② Are there any side effects? 這個藥有副作用嗎？

131 How many of these tablets should I take?
我要吃幾個藥片呢？

132 When do I take them? 藥什麼時候服用呢？

133 How do I take this? 要如何服用呢？

134 Please take it when you feel severe pain.
只有在很痛的時候才要服用。

135 Please take it if the symptoms get worse.
只有症狀嚴重的時候才要服用。

136 Please take it three times a day, after every meal.
一天三次，餐後服用。

137 Please take it twice a day, in the morning and evening.
一天兩次，早、晚服用。

138 Please take it once a day, before you go to bed.
一天一次，睡前服用。

DIALOGUE

Ⓐ I left my bag on the train.

Ⓑ Which train was it?

Ⓐ It was the train that just left. I was in a car toward the front of the train.

Ⓑ What kind of bag is it?

Ⓐ A small brown bag. It's made of leather.

Ⓑ What do you have in it?

Ⓐ My wallet, passport, traveler's checks, and personal effects.

Ⓐ 我的皮包放在火車上，忘記拿了。

Ⓑ 是哪一班車呢？

Ⓐ 就是剛開走的那班車，我剛剛坐在那班車的前面車廂裡。

Ⓑ 是什麼樣的皮包？

Ⓐ 是咖啡色的真皮皮包。

Ⓑ 裡面有什麼東西？

Ⓐ 有我的錢包、護照、旅行支票，和一些私人物品。

Study Points

It was the train that just left.	就在剛開走的列車上。	just left 指剛剛發班的火車
a car toward the front of the train	前面的車廂	某節車廂的說法是： I was in the third car from the front (/back). 我在前面（／後面）的第三節車廂
It's made of . . .	是……質材的	「be made of . . .」指 「由……製造而成」

在海外旅遊，可能會遇到搶劫、遺失護照或貴重物品，或是遇到交通事故等情況，所以要如何預防，或是遇到問題時該怎麼處理，這些都是重要的課題。

最常發生的情況是遇到扒手，所以出門時，最好不要帶太多錢，並且隨時留意自己身邊的東西，尤其是在國外，如果花錢時表現出很有錢的樣子，就很容易為歹徒所覬覦。所以，為了怕發生搶劫、車禍或是生病，出國前最好先投保海外旅遊平安險。

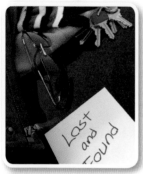

1 lost and found 行李遺失招領處

2 police station 警察局

3 police car 警車

4 policeman 員警

5 embassy 大使館

6 consulate 領事館

I'd like to report the theft as follows. Please make the certificate of the theft.

VICTIM	/	/	/
FAMILY NAME			
DATE OF BIRTH		GIVEN NANE	
NATIONALITY		DAY / MONTH / YEAR	/ /
ADDRESS			
ADDRESS IN THIS COUNTRY			

DATE OF THEFT

DATE / MONTH / YEAR / AM. / PM. /

PLACE OF THEFT
- ☐ ON THE STREET
- ☐ IN THE SUBWAY ☐ AT THE STATION
- ☐ IN THE TAXI ☐ IN THE TRAIN/BUS
- ☐ AT THE HOTEL ☐ IN THE LOBBY ☐ AT THE AIRPORT
- ☐ AT THE SHOP ☐ IN THE ROOM ☐ OTHER
- ☐ AT THE MUSEUM ☐ AT RESTAURANT/BAR
- ☐ OTHER PLACE:

TYPES OF THEFT
- ☐ BAGGAGE THEFT ☐ PICKPOCKET
- ☐ BY MOTORBIKE ☐ BY PICK ☐ EXTORTION
- GUN

7 lost item report 遺失證明

8 theft report 失竊證明

9 missing items report 遺失證明

10 **reissue** 重新申請

11 **traffic accident** 交通事故

12 **ambulance** 救護車

13 **witness** 目擊證人

14 **damage** 損傷

15 **injured person** 傷患

16 **driver's license** 駕照

17 **license number** 牌照號碼

18 **speed limit** 限速

1 遺失東西

1 I've lost my wallet. 我的錢包掉了。

2 My wallet is missing. 我的錢包不見了。

3 I dropped my purse somewhere. 我的錢包不知掉在哪裡了。

4 I think I left my wallet in your shop.
我的錢包好像放在你們的店裡，忘記拿走了。

5 It's a red leather wallet. 它是個紅色的皮包。

6 I'm not sure where I left it. 我不太確定它掉到哪裡去了。

7 I left my bag in the taxi. 我把包包留在計程車上忘記拿了。

8 Do you remember the name of the taxi company?
你知道是哪家公司的計程車嗎？

9 I left my briefcase on the train. 我把公事包遺留在火車上了。

10 Have you seen a bag about this size?
你有沒有看過大約這個大小的皮包呢？

wallet 皮夾子

purse 錢包

fanny pack 霹靂包

handbag 手提包

briefcase 公事包

suitcase 皮箱

sports bag 運動包

backpack 後背包

luggage 行李箱

2 失竊時 🎧97

11 My wallet was stolen. 我的錢包被偷了。

12 I lost my wallet with my credit card.
我放有信用卡的錢包被偷了。

13 Somebody picked my pocket. 我的東西被扒走了。

14 I had my wallet stolen from my pocket on the train.
我的錢包在火車上被偷了。

15 A man snatched my bag on the street.
我的包包在街上被一個男人搶走了。

16 My camera was stolen while I was away from my room.
我離開房間後，我的照相機就被偷了。

17 Would you call the police right now?
你可以馬上幫我叫警察嗎？

18
Ⓐ Hello. Front desk. May I help you?
Ⓑ I think someone broke into my room.
Ⓐ 您好，這裡是櫃檯，可以為您效勞嗎？
Ⓑ 我的房間好像有人闖進來。

19
Ⓐ What was taken from your room?
Ⓑ A ring and a watch.
Ⓐ 你遺失了什麼東西？
Ⓑ 一只戒指和一支手錶。

3 申報遺失

20 Where is the lost and found? 失物招領中心在哪裡？

21 Where is the nearest police station? 最近的警察局在哪裡？

22 Please fill out a missing items report. 請填寫這張遺失清單。

23 I'd like to report a theft. 我想要報失竊案。

24 I'd like to report a stolen wallet. 我的皮包被偷了，要報案。

25 Could you fill out a theft report form?
請開失竊證明書給我。

26
Ⓐ What was stolen?
Ⓑ I was robbed of my handbag in front of the hotel near here.
Ⓐ 什麼東西被偷了？
Ⓑ 在這附近的飯店前面，我的手提包被搶了。

27
Ⓐ What kind of a handbag is it?
Ⓑ It's a black leather handbag.
Ⓐ 是什麼樣的手提包？
Ⓑ 是一個黑色的皮製手提包。

28
Ⓐ What did you have in it?
Ⓑ Passport, traveler's checks, and some cash.
Ⓐ 你的皮包裡有什麼？
Ⓑ 裡面有我的護照、旅行支票，還有一點現金。

29

A How much money were you carrying?

B One hundred dollars in cash, 300 dollars in traveler's checks, and my credit card.

A 裡面有多少錢？

B 有現金100塊和300塊旅行支票，還有信用卡。

30 I had my wallet taken from my pocket. 我的錢包被扒走了。

31 Could you fill out this form? 麻煩你填寫這張表格。

32 Please call my hotel as soon as you find it.
尋獲的話，請盡速打電話到飯店與我聯絡。

4 遺失護照

33 I've lost my passport. 我的護照掉了。

34 I left my passport somewhere. 我不知道護照放在哪裡了。

35 I'd like to report a lost passport.
我的護照遺失了，我想報案。

36 What papers do I need to get a new passport?
申請新護照需要準備哪些文件？

37 Where is the Taiwanese Embassy [Taiwanese Consulate]?
台灣大使館〔台灣領事館〕在哪裡？

38 Can you give me the telephone number of the Taiwanese Embassy? 你可以幫我查台灣大使館的電話號碼嗎？

REISSUE
申請補辦

在國外旅遊，如果物品遭竊或遺失，都是一件掃興的事。但如果不幸發生，該如何將損失降到最低呢？

在出國之前，先影印所有文件，一份留給家人，一份隨身攜帶，但要與正本分開。如此一來，萬一不幸遇到什麼事情，就能將不便的程度減到最低。以下介紹幾種貴重物品遺失時的補辦手續。

遺失護照

先到警察局辦理「失竊證明」（Report of Theft）或是「遺失證明」（Report of Loss），這樣就不用擔心有人冒用身分。

之後，再憑證明文件至本國駐外大使館或代表處補辦護照。

如果出發前準備好護照影本，就可以省去多項手續。

遺失旅行支票

旅行支票的購票證明最好與正本分開存放，並記下支票號碼。

如果有購票證明或支票號碼，到銀行時將可直接申請補發，甚至只需要一通電話即可完成手續，並在短時間內取得補發的支票。

遺失信用卡

為避免信用卡遭盜刷，最好能立即通知發卡銀行，要求停卡或是掛失。

某些發卡銀行甚至可以在短時間內補發新卡，並送至你手上。

遺失機票

須立即通知航空公司，告知班機時間等資料。

大部份航空公司很少能立即補發臨時機票，而是要求旅客先買另一張機票，並將原機票作廢，日後再退還原機票的款項。

39 What's the telephone number for the Taiwanese Embassy? 台灣大使館的電話號碼是幾號？

40 I lost my traveler's checks. 我的旅行支票掉了。

41 These are the check numbers. 這是支票的號碼。

42 Where should I apply for reissue?
重新申請要在哪裡辦手續？

43 Can you reissue them? 可以重新申請嗎？

44 Here is the purchase agreement. 這是購買證明。

45 How long does it take to have them reissued?
重新申請要花多久時間？

46 I've lost my credit card. 我的信用卡掉了。

47 Can you cancel my card number, please?
我要將信用卡作廢。

48 I'd like to get a new card. 我要申請新的信用卡。

5 請求幫助 (100)

49 Help! 救命啊！

50 Police! 警察！

51 Thief! 小偷啊！

52 Robber! 搶劫啊！

53 Stop him! 抓住他！

54 A man is following me! 有個男人一直跟著我！

55 Fire! 失火了啊！

56 Call the police! 快報警啊！

57 Call an ambulance! 叫救護車！

58 Operator, get me the fire station! 總機，幫我接消防隊。

國人在海外遭遇急難時，如何尋求駐外館處協助？

我國於世界各地共設有一百多個駐外單位，均設置有「急難救助專線電話」，國人於海外需要駐外館處協助時，請於上班時間逕撥最近駐外館處辦公室電話，非上班時間則請撥急難救助專線電話或行動電話。駐外館處地址、電話和急難救助專線電話，均載於「中華民國駐外館處緊急聯絡電話暨通訊錄」，該通訊錄於機場出境大廳或服務台及本局與分支機構大廳，均可免費取用。

此外，國內親友也可直接與「外交部緊急聯絡中心」聯繫，電話為0800-085-095，該中心 24 小時服務。

一般護照遺失或被竊案件，請先向當地警察局報案並取得報案證明。通常，駐外館處僅能在上班時間，依據報案證明，補辦護照或核發返國旅行文件。

駐外館處提供旅外國人服務事項，可參閱「中華民國駐外館處提供旅外國人服務項目」。此外，外交部領事事務局亦編有「出國旅行安全實用手冊」，該小冊同樣可於機場出境大廳或服務台及本局與分支機構大廳免費取得，建議出國時隨身攜帶，以備不時之需。

6 交通事故

59 I had a traffic accident. 我發生車禍了。

60 Someone's been injured. 有人受傷了。

61 My friend is seriously injured! 我的朋友傷得很嚴重。

62 Please send an ambulance! 請派一輛救護車過來。

63 Where is the telephone booth? 哪裡有公用電話？

64 Can you take me to a hospital? 請帶我去醫院。

65 I was within the speed limit. 我是在速限內。

66 The other car suddenly changed lanes. 對方突然變換車道。

67 It wasn't my fault. 這不是我的過失。

68 Please give me a copy of the accident report.
請給我車禍證明書。

69 I'm insured against the accident. 我有投保意外險。

collision 碰撞

rear-end collision 尾端衝撞

chain collision 連環車禍

serious injury 重傷

slight injury 輕傷

外交部
緊急聯絡
中心

為加強提供國人旅外急難服務，成立「外交部緊急聯絡中心」，24 小時全年無休，電話為：

國內免付費　0800-085-095（諧音：您幫我・您救我）
海外付費　　（當地國的國際碼）+886-800-085-095

國人在海外遭遇緊急危難時，可透過該專線電話尋求聯繫協助。非涉及海外急難救助事項，切勿撥打該專線電話，以免線路過度負載，耽誤海外緊急事故處理時效。

倘有護照、簽證及文件證明等問題，請於上班時間撥打外交部領事事務局，總機電話：(02) 2343-2888

外交部一般業務查詢，請於上班時間撥打外交部，總機電話：(02) 2348-2999

中心另設有「旅外國人急難救助全球免付費專線」，目前可適用歐、美、日、韓、澳洲等 22 個國家或地區，電話為：
800-0885-0885（諧音：您幫幫我、您幫幫我）

中國大陸地區請撥打「海基會緊急服務專線」，電話為：
(02) 2533-9995

國家圖書館出版品預行編目資料

說著英文去旅行 /Carlos Campbell 著. -- 初版.
--[臺北市]：寂天文化 , 2019.04　面；　　公
分

ISBN 978-986-318-094-4(20K 平裝附光碟片)
ISBN 978-986-318-265-8(20K 精裝附光碟片)
ISBN 978-986-318-168-2(32K 平裝附光碟片)
ISBN 978-986-318-446-1(32K 精裝附光碟片)
ISBN 978-986-318-647-2(50K 平裝附光碟片)
ISBN 978-986-318-792-9(25K 平裝附光碟片)

1. 英語　2. 旅遊　3. 會話

805.188　　　　　　　　　　　　108004237

作者	Carlos Campbell
審訂者	Judy Majewski
校對	陳慧莉
製程管理	洪巧玲
出版者	寂天文化事業股份有限公司
電話	+886-(0)2-2365-9739
傳真	+886-(0)2-2365-9835
網址	www.icosmos.com.tw
讀者服務	onlineservice@icosmos.com.tw
出版日期	2019 年 4 月　　初版六刷　　250101
郵撥帳號	1998620-0　寂天文化事業股份有限公司

訂購金額 600 （含）元以上郵資免費

訂購金額 600 元以下者，請外加郵資 65 元

若有破損，請寄回更換